DEAD OF A COUNTERPLOT
SIMON NASH

Dead of a Counterplot

Simon Nash

PERENNIAL LIBRARY
Harper & Row, Publishers
New York, Cambridge, Philadelphia, San Francisco
London, Mexico City, São Paulo, Singapore, Sydney

This book is fiction. All characters and incidents are entirely imaginary.

A hardcover edition of this book was published in England by Geoffrey Bles Ltd. It is here reprinted by arrangement with the author.

DEAD OF A COUNTERPLOT. Copyright © 1962 by Simon Nash. All rights reserved. Printed in the United States of America. No part of this book may be used or reproduced in any manner whatsoever without written permission except in the case of brief quotations embodied in critical articles and reviews. For information address Harper & Row, Publishers, Inc., 10 East 53rd Street, New York, N.Y. 10022. Published simultaneously in Canada by Fitzhenry & Whiteside Limited, Toronto.

First PERENNIAL LIBRARY edition published 1985.

Library of Congress Cataloging in Publication Data

Dead of a counterplot.

"Perennial Library."
Reprint. Originally published: London : G. Bles, 1962.
I. Title.
PR 6005.H323D38   1985   823'.914   84-48613
ISBN 0-06-080757-1 (pbk.)

85 86 87 88 89 10 OPM 9 8 7 6 5 4 3 2

DEAD OF A COUNTERPLOT

CHAPTER I

When Bernard Mudge was a student at North London College towards the end of the last century, the authorities were far from looking on him as a potential benefactor. After failing for the second time to get any sort of a pass in the B.A. (General) degree, he left the University of London and all its works behind him and entered his father's brewery. Since two wars and increasing taxation failed to quench the thirst of Londoners, he prospered so greatly that the legend "Mudge's is Marvellous" appeared everywhere on hoardings and public transport. Yet his years at North London College must have held for him a charm that his lecturers had never suspected, for gifts came often and richly from him as the profits of the brewery increased. When he died in 1947, a widower without children, there was a good deal of speculation in the Senior Common Room about what his will would produce. For dons are worldly men, who sometimes lift their eyes to look around and see what the great chance is bringing them. A professor will thrust his department forward like a beloved but needy child when there is talk of bequests and benefactions. What Bernard Mudge did in fact leave to his old college was a singularly hideous house in Hampstead, built by his grandfather who had founded the firm, and enlarged by the succeeding generations of Mudges. The terms of the bequest were clear. The house was to be used as a Hall of Residence for male students of the college and was to be known for all time as Mudge Hall.

"It's not quite what we would have chosen," said the Warden some twelve years later, "but we were lucky to get it when we did."

Arthur Blake was launched again on his pet theme. In the chair opposite him, Adam Ludlow took another sip of his whisky and listened without enthusiasm to the late October rain beating against the window. The two men were brought together less by any real kinship of spirit or interest than by the fact of being bachelors who were well past forty and had come to realise that they were unlikely to make much more progress in their careers. Too old to mix easily with the younger lecturers, not senior enough to call together their own respectful circle, they fell into each other's company as soon as the long vacation was over. Blake, short and tubby, with a fringe of fair hair at the back of his prematurely bald head, peered over his glasses as if in continual surprise at having got as far as he had. He was warden of Mudge Hall mainly because he had been the only bachelor on the staff of the college at that time who was a suitable age for the post. He had never really understood his students, but felt that he was some-how doing a useful job. Adam Ludlow, on the other hand, carried his tall, thin body with a stoop of perpetual irritation at not having got farther than he had. He could have been a brilliant scholar, and he knew it. He could have been near the final step to a chair of English, instead of being shunted off down the branch line that leads to the buffers of a Senior Lectureship. The combination of a small private income, a diversity of non-academic interests and a lazy nature would keep him where he was. Knowing his own ability, he fluctuated between inordinate pride in each

8

new achievement and abysmal self-depreciation at each new setback. He was also clear-sighted enough to recognise his own moods. Now he half closed his deep, grey eyes under their rugged brows and sympathetically nodded his untidy head while he wondered whether he could decently hang on until the rain eased a little.

"Yes, they certainly are a handful," Blake was saying with that air of mingled pride and despair with which wardens habitually regard their flocks.

"They seem quiet enough tonight," said Ludlow.

"It's early yet—only twenty to eleven. Saturday always brings them back late. We'll hear them all right, later on."

"I ought to go," said Ludlow without conviction.

"Don't move, my dear fellow. One develops a kind of sixth sense about which noises are significant. Anyway, Latham's in charge tonight. We do alternate week-ends, and he won't call me unless there's an emergency—which there never is. Let him cope."

Stuart Latham, Blake's sub-warden, was at that moment coping with the biggest emergency that he or anyone else in Mudge Hall had ever had to face. Five minutes before, he had had a knock on his door from Tom Ferris, the night porter.

"Excuse me, sir," said Tom, thrusting round the door his face that always gave the impression of being half-shaved, "but there's something you ought to know."

This was a well-known introduction to trouble. Latham groaned and murmured, "Well?"

"It's Mr. Trent. He had that girl in earlier this evening —you know, the one what's a Commie, and she hasn't come out. She was going to see him, and I put her in the book, but he hasn't been along since to sign her out."

9

"Are you sure, Ferris? I don't want to go down for nothing."

"Now Mr. Latham, sir, have you ever known me to make any mistake when it was a matter of discipline?"

Latham was tempted to refer to the time when Tom had roused him at two in the morning with the report that there was a girl in the Hall, only to track down the distinctive high-pitched laugh of an African student. He said nothing, but got up and followed the porter down to the next floor. All seemed quiet. Ominously quiet, thought Latham. He went to the door marked 27, Tom in watchful attendance behind him like a sergeant ready to take any man's name at the Orderly Officer's command. Latham knocked on the door. No answer. He knocked again, louder.

"Trent, are you there?"

Silence. Latham rattled the door.

"It's the Sub-Warden. Please open the door, Trent."

He turned to the patient Tom.

"He must have taken her out."

"I'll swear he hasn't. He hasn't signed her out in the book." Latham was on the point of giving up. Then he decided it was time that Tom Ferris was put in his place and taught to be more careful.

"I'm going up to get the master-key," he said. "If the room is empty, I shall tell the Warden that you brought me out for nothing." Tom made a noise between a snort and an apologetic grunt, and stood back while Latham stamped back upstairs, to return a minute later with a key in his hand. He went to the door, and knocked again.

"Trent, I'm going to open this door: I insist on coming in." Still silence. Only the rain caught up in a flurry of wind on the other side of the house. Tom Ferris urged him on.

"She's still there," he said, "I'll stake my reputation on it." Latham put the key in the lock and threw open the door. Tom's reputation was safe. Jenny Hexham was there, and would not leave it for any rule of discipline that was ever made.

Ludlow had just decided that he could not politely stay any longer when there was a knock on Blake's door that seemed to be caused by the impact of a whole body rather than a set of knuckles. This impression was confirmed immediately when the door burst open and a red-haired man of about thirty fell rather than stepped into the room.

"Ah, Latham," said Blake with the air of a man who has long ceased to be surprised at anything. "You know our colleague Ludlow in the English Department, I hope —though the staff is such a size nowadays that one can't guarantee knowing people any more; Latham is my Sub-Warden, Ludlow . . ."

"She's dead," squeaked Latham, "murdered. That boy Trent must have done it. Horrible. Come quickly. Get the police."

"Calm yourself, my dear fellow," said Blake, giving him a glass of whisky, "what has young Trent been up to now? He's one of yours, isn't he?" he added to Ludlow, rather accusingly.

"Robert Trent? Yes, he's one of my finalists. A very good lad too. What's the trouble?"

Latham expanded his previous disjointed remarks. Blake seemed inclined to disbelieve him, taking the line that they were always up to something, especially on Saturdays.

"But," he added thoughtfully, "you say she's still in the room? That won't do—it's well after ten-thirty. All guests must go."

"She can't go," said Latham helplessly, "she's dead."

"Nonsense. Perfectly healthy girl. I expect she's fainted. Better tell Matron, and leave it to her."

"I think we ought to go over," said Ludlow.

The Warden's flat was across the courtyard from the other wing, but they were spared the need of going out in the rain by a covered bridge. By the time they arrived, the corridor outside room 27 was no longer so peaceful. Several students were clustered around the doorway, held back by Tom who seemed quite unperturbed by the whole thing. They made way for Blake and Ludlow; Latham seemed unwilling to enter the room again.

It was not a large room. The area considered suitable for a student to work and sleep is not large. Being in his third year, Trent had one of the better rooms in the Hall, but it still gave little floor-space among the furniture. The body of Jenny Hexham seemed disproportionately large, sprawled on the hearth-rug in front of the gas-fire. The little crowd in the doorway could see that she had been strangled with the orange silk scarf that she wore. Her handbag lay open by her head, its contents spilt out on the rug. She lay face upwards, her left arm by her side, her right arm thrown out towards the open window as if in a last indication of the way her killer had gone. The window was wide open. The wind, blowing against the other side of the building, had not disturbed the curtains, which hung straight down as if they had just been drawn. The fire-escape from the room, a complicated affair of webbing and canvas which was fixed above the window, had been unfastened and hung down into the darkness. An upright chair was overturned behind the door, but there was no other sign that any struggle had taken place. The untidy divan-bed, the desk with scattered notes for an essay, the bookcase beside it—all looked as any student's room might be expected to look. The gas-fire was lit but turned down low.

Blake stood in the middle of the room, refusing to believe that such a thing had happened in his Hall and still inclined to regard the whole affair as a misunderstanding. Ludlow waited for an instant to take in the whole scene, then moved with a speed that surprised those who knew his usual lethargic movements. In two strides he was at the window, looking down into the courtyard. He then studied the fire-escape. It was one of those devices by which people can descend alternately from a height. There are two lengths of canvas, each with a sling at the end. The first man goes down, his descent controlled by a spring in the body of the apparatus, and when the second one follows him the first sling is drawn up again. This movement is repeated as often as may be necessary. Ludlow laid his hand on the sling which hung limp and empty in the window. Then he bent down by Jenny Hexham and felt her wrist.

"Get a doctor," he said to the gaping group in the doorway, "though I'm afraid it's too late. And telephone to the police."

For a moment nobody moved. Everyone looked at the Warden.

"It will cause a scandal," said Blake. "This is the sort of thing that gets us a bad name."

It is to be feared that being Warden of a Hall of Residence tends to limit one's standards of morality. Ludlow knelt by Jenny, pulling loose the scarf round her neck.

"I say, don't you think you ought to leave that until the police come?"

The speaker was a tall, plump young man with straight

fair hair brushed up in front. Ludlow gave him one of his famous looks, usually reserved for those who suggested that Bacon was Shakespeare, or that Pope was not a true poet.

"If you did something about calling the police, it would be more useful than interfering with a work of mercy."

He began artificial respiration. Henry Prentice, the student who had spoken, went away, followed by Tom Ferris. Another voice was heard from the doorway, this time with a strong foreign accent:

"Leave her alone. It is better that she should be dead. She was a bad woman."

And an English voice answered him with a note of hysteria, "You swine, what do you know about it?" The new speaker pushed his way into the room; he seemed on the verge of tears. "Let me come in," he said, "I'm her cousin."

Blake was moved at last from his inaction by having a student to deal with.

"I'm sorry, Hexham, but there seems to be nothing you can do. We must wait for the police."

Michael Hexham knelt down opposite Ludlow. He looked at his cousin's distorted face and shuddered. Then he ran to the window and looked out. Suddenly he turned again to the body on the floor. His normally high-pitched voice rose to a scream, as he pointed first at Ludlow, then at the group in the doorway:

"Her bracelet—he's stolen her bracelet."

CHAPTER II

Without any of them actually saying it, Blake, Latham and
Ludlow decided that they had better stay together until the
police came. Dr. Hastings, who regularly attended the Hall,
lived only a few doors away and came at once. He having
quickly declared Ludlow's efforts to be useless, the three
men were not sorry to leave him with the body while they
withdrew to Latham's rooms on the floor above. Henry
Prentice fulfilled one of the ambitions of every student by
dialling 999 and calling Scotland Yard. Within a very short
time, Tom Ferris was showing in two police officers.

"Good evening, gentlemen," said the first. "I am Inspector Montero: Spanish descent, a long time back. This
is Detective-Sergeant Jack Springer."

"Known in the Force as Spring-heeled Jack." Springer
took up his cue with an alacrity that made the two men
sound like a pair of cross-talk comedians.

But there was nothing comic about Montero. Barely
reaching regulation height, he had worked up from the
beat to an inspectorship in the C.I.D. against the expectations of all who knew him. His mild blue eyes seemed con-
tinually astonished at the wickedness of the world. His soft
voice, still with a trace of the West Country that he had
left many years ago, seemed fitter to speak of cattle-fairs
and harvest prospects than of London crime. His close,
fair moustache made his mouth and slightly receding chin
look even gentler and more simple. But those eyes had

made the bolder eyes of some very tough characters drop their gaze, and the soft voice had often uttered a well-deserved doom. Nobody made the mistake of under-estimating Herbert Montero more than once. Springer was tall, thin and saturnine, with a rather frightened look. He, too, greatly belied his appearance.

Blake made the necessary introductions. Montero greeted each of them with cordiality and respect. Then he launched his first question like a jet-propelled icicle.

"And which of you three interfered with the body?"

Ludlow admitted his guilt and was given a short lecture on the need for leaving everything in a case like this just as you found it.

"Perhaps you'll remember that next time," Montero concluded.

"I hope there won't be any next time," said Ludlow sadly.

"You never know your luck," said Springer, who until then had apparently been taking a profound interest in Latham's Picasso reproduction.

"I'm afraid my thought was to act from humanity rather than the letter of the law," said Ludlow and then cursed himself for sounding pompous. He added, "She was still warm. I thought there might have been a chance of recovering her."

"How much damage you've done to the case remains to be seen," said Montero gently. "I've got a couple of men in the room taking pictures and dabs, so until they finish perhaps you gentlemen will help me to fill in some of the background."

"Dabs?" asked Blake anxiously, wondering what else had got into the Hall that night.

"Fingerprints. By the way, I've got a man on the front door too. No other way out, I suppose?"

"Not officially. I've a shrewd idea that they have ways of getting in and out after the door's shut." Blake looked as if he regarded his possession of this knowledge as being very shrewd indeed.

"Well, anybody who tries that tonight lays himself open to suspicion."

Blake looked glassy-eyed at the thought of dozens of his students climbing in, to be seized by burly policemen and charged with murder. Montero coughed encouragingly. Springer opened his notebook and looked from one to the other like a hopeful spaniel.

"What can you tell me about the dead girl?" asked Montero. "Was she a resident here?"

"Good heavens, no: this is a hall for male students. All guests must leave by ten p.m.—ten-thirty on Saturdays." Blake seemed to draw some comfort from quoting the rules.

"I see. Do you happen to know her address?"

"No. I think she came from the Midlands, but I don't know where she was lodging in London. I expect one of the students will know."

"She was a frequent visitor here, then?"

"Well, she was in quite a lot."

"What sort of a young woman would you say she was?"

"I don't know anything about her, except that she seemed to know a lot of the students here. Mr. Ludlow can probably tell you more about her."

All eyes turned to Ludlow, who folded his hands and looked as if he was about to dictate a testimonial.

"Third-years honours' student," he said. "Not first-class material, but could be on the way to an upper second if she worked, which she doesn't—er, didn't. Better on the linguistic side than the literary, and that's unusual for a woman."

"Do you know anything about her outside interests?" asked Montero. "What sort of things she did in the evening, what friends she had, and so on?"

"If student gossip is to be believed, the things she did in the evening are better passed over lightly."

"You mean she had a bad reputation with men?"

"A good reputation with men, so to speak. Bad probably with the other girls. Those at least whose natural disadvantages lead them to believe that the virtue of compulsory chastity can be made to atone for sins of slander, pride and envy——"

"Compound for sins they are inclined to,

By damning those they have no mind to," interrupted Montero.

"Eh?" Ludlow was for once put off his stroke.

"*Hudibras*—Samuel Butler, you know."

"Yes," said Ludlow. "I know, but I didn't expect you would." He looked at Montero with a new respect, and dropping his donnish manner, suddenly became business-like.

"But you want to know about Jenny Hexham. I suppose her political activities took up a good deal of her time that might have been better employed——"

"May I ask what kind of politics?"

"You may. She was the leader of the small but vocal Communist group in College."

"Was she, indeed!" Both Montero and Springer looked interested.

"Good heavens," said Blake, "I never knew that. Do you think she got any of my chaps mixed up in it?"

"I'm afraid she did—Robert Trent for one."

18

"Oh dear!"

"Can we go back a bit?" asked Montero. "Do you know of any enemies this girl might have had, among the students?"

"I imagine she aroused fairly strong passions, in more senses than one. I don't know anybody who wanted to kill her."

"But these Communist activities of hers that you spoke of. They can often lead these young—er—intellectuals among undesirable people, before they know what they're really doing. Did she have any regular callers who weren't students?"

"There I can't help you. They certainly didn't call at any of her tutorials with me. You'd better ask at her lodgings."

"We'll do that in good time." Montero was becoming a little impatient. "Now about this young man Robert Trent, who you mentioned just now. I think it was in his room that the body was found?"

"Yes, that's right," said Latham, who had been apparently in a state of suspended animation for some time. "I went there when the porter told me that this girl hadn't gone out—they have to go by ten-thirty on Saturdays—and there she was." He relapsed into gloom again.

"Thank you, sir. I'll have your full story later. At present I'm just interested in the general background. I'd like to know a bit more about Mr. Trent."

"He's good," said Ludlow. "One of my best third-year men. Quite an unusual distinction of style. I suppose this business will put him off for months, but he ought to have got a first. It will be that girl's fault if he doesn't——"

"Quite so. Do I understand that he and Miss Hexham were studying the same subject?"

"They were reading for the same honours school; yes."

"I stand rebuked," said Montero.

Ludlow, who like many men with ready sarcasm never really wanted to upset anybody, had the grace to blush. Montero took advantage of his embarrassment to put another question.

"Do you think Mr. Trent was in any way involved with her politics?"

"I said just now that he was," said Ludlow, "and you'd better hear the whole story from me before you get it from anybody else and start suspecting him of killing her. Trent went to eastern Europe at the end of his first year, in the vacation—one of those Communist places, I forget which. He went with one of those half-baked student tours. You know, the sort where they sleep in railway sidings because somebody loses the name of the town they're going to——"

"Exactly," said Montero, who was used to digressive witnesses but was finding Ludlow exceptionally difficult.

"Well, he got there," went on Ludlow happily, "and came back. Then these people started following him up—asking him to parties at their embassy and so on. You may not know it, but they've got an extremely elaborate system for getting hold of people who show the least interest——"

"Yes, we know all about that. Anyway, Special Branch does, and we know all we need to know. So young Trent became a Communist?"

"Certainly not. He was flattered and excited by their attention, I suppose, and perhaps he got in a bit deeper than he intended. But he's got too much sense to do anything really silly. That girl Jenny was a real Bolshie—dyed red in the wool, so to speak, and she'd got her claws into him. She was clever, no doubt of that."

"What was the nature of their relationship?"

"If you mean, was he sleeping with her, I don't think so. You wouldn't encourage it here anyway, eh, Blake?"

"Bless my soul, no. Nothing like that happens here, Inspector."

"I'm glad to hear it, sir. Now I think the sooner we can get a word with Mr. Trent the better; though from what we've seen and heard so far he may be difficult to find. And then I'd like to talk to some of those gentlemen who got to the scene of the crime when you did. I suppose this building is full of students—how many altogether?"

"Eighty-five," said Blake, "though only twenty live in this block. As it's Saturday, I expect most of them were out when she was—when it happened. They all go off to dances, and so on. I imagine those whom we saw would be about the only ones here."

"What time do they all have to be in?"

"Midnight. We shut the door at ten and they can't go out after that but they can come in till twelve."

Blake's experience of Saturday evenings proved to be right. There were few students who had been anywhere near the room, and these were soon identified and asked to wait for questioning. Montero and Springer established themselves in the secretary's office on the ground floor, after a few words with Dr. Hastings. The doctor, an elderly, laconic Scot, could tell them that death was the result of strangulation and had taken place about half past ten.

"Which means," said Montero, "that the murderer was probably in the room when Latham first came to the door."

"And panicked and went out through the window," Springer said. "A pity Mr. Latham wasn't quicker with his keys—might have saved us a lot of trouble. Not that there seems to be much difficulty with this. Who else but Trent could have been in that room?"

"That's what we've got to find out," said Montero, who knew from experience that his subordinate's apparent impetuosity was often a careful thinking-out of the evidence. "Let's have a look at this porter chap first."

Tom Ferris was very willing to give evidence. He had been on duty at his desk in the entrance-hall since six o'clock, leaving it only to have his supper at eight and to stoke the boiler at ten.

"How long were you away after ten?" Montero asked him.

"About ten minutes more or less, rather less than more. They're awkward old things those boilers, and you can't hurry the stoking. It's time they got new ones."

"Yes, yes. Now think carefully; who did you see entering or leaving the building this evening?"

"Plenty leaving, it being a Saturday. Not many came in, though. There was that girl of course, the one what's been done in—*and* I can't say I'm sorry."

"Really? Why aren't you sorry?"

"She was always hanging around here, now to see this one, now that one. Couldn't leave them alone. And she was a Commie, which I don't hold with. Conservative me, and always have been, like my poor father before me——"

"What time did she come this evening?"

"Half past eight exactly. Just as I'd got back from my supper, and I'm never a minute over time."

"And she asked for Mr. Trent?"

"Never asked for nobody. That was her way, to walk in as if she owned the place. Hussy! But *I* asked *her*, and she had to say it was Mr. Trent again."

"She often came to see him?"

"Every night almost, since this term started—and he ought to know better. A nice young gentleman, and expected to do well if he'd keep to his studies and not go confolating about."

Montero was so charmed by this participle that he had to stop and be sure Springer had made an exact note of it. Then he asked Tom to go on with his account of the evening.

"Nothing much else, except the students going out in twos and threes to their dances and things. Nothing that I remember—only that Pole coming for his key."

"Who?"

"Steve what's-'is-name—never can pronounce it. He'd locked himself out, as they're always doing and giving me extra work. So he came for the master-key to get in."

"What time was that?"

"Just on ten—minute before I went to do the boilers."

"And when did he bring the key back?"

"While I was away—dropped them down on the desk and ran off the way they do. It's a wonder we don't all get murdered in our beds, they're that careless with keys."

"What happened then?"

"I put the keys away. Half past ten, *she* hadn't gone, so I said to myself, it's time for a word with Mr. Latham—he being in charge for the evening."

"Why were you so sure she hadn't gone? Couldn't she have left while you were away from your desk?"

"Because I sign the guest in, and the student who had her signs her out, with the time. Mr. Trent hadn't put nothing in the book."

"I see. Thank you, that will do for now. I wonder if you could bring in one of the students we asked to wait in the room down the corridor. There are three of them—any one will do."

When Tom had gone, Montero looked whimsically at Springer.

"Do you think these porters have microphones in every room?" he said.

"They're the ones for gossip, all right," said Springer, "and I wouldn't be surprised if that one knows more than he said."

His conjectures were cut short by the return of Tom with Henry Prentice, who looked as if he was determined that no policemen were going to get the better of him.

"What is your full name?" asked Montero.

"Henry Albert Prentice."

"You are a student?"

"Yes, of course. I wouldn't be in this Hall if I wasn't."

"We have to establish these facts formally."

"Quite so. Well, I'm a post-graduate student of chemistry. I graduated last session and am now working for my M.Sc."

"Thank you. Now, Mr. Prentice, I believe you were in the vicinity of room 27 when the body of Jenny Hexham was discovered there."

"Yes. I heard a lot of banging and the Sub-Warden shouting outside Robert's room, so I went up to see what was happening."

"Is it far from your own room?"

"Mine is directly underneath. And besides——"

"Yes, Mr. Prentice?"

"I don't want to say anything that would get anybody into trouble."

"I think you'd better tell us everything you know. If you have any information that can throw light on this affair, it will certainly have to come out eventually. Anything you tell me that has no relevance to the crime will be completely confidential."

"I see. Perhaps it will be best if I tell you all about this evening."

"Please do."

"Well, Robert came down to see me——"

"Excuse my interrupting you, but Robert is Mr. Robert Trent who occupies room 27?"

"Yes."

"Is he a friend of yours?"

"We get on pretty well. Not close friends, but he's always tended to confide in me—treats me as a sort of father-figure. It sounds a bit conceited, but you know what I mean. I'm a year senior to him, and that can make a lot of difference to a young chap like Robert."

"May I ask how old you are, Mr. Prentice?"

"Twenty-three. I know you're laughing up your sleeve, but Robert is very young for his age—immature, in a way. But I was telling you, he came to my room, very upset because he'd been having a row with Jenny."

"Did you yourself know Miss Hexham?"

"Not terribly well. She was quite a college character—ran the Communists and all that. She was always around the Hall."

"So I've gathered. What time did Mr. Trent come to see you?"

"Quarter-past nine. I know, because I'd just finished listening to a broadcast I was interested in. He'd been getting mixed up with the Communists—I don't know how much you know about this."

Montero did not speak.

"Anyway, Jenny had rather got her claws into him.

I don't know quite what she was up to, but apparently she was trying to drag him in deeper. Robert wanted to pull out, but she was threatening him that she had evidence of things he'd done already, things that might cause trouble for him——" He stopped short again.

"Please go on," said Montero. "Sergeant Springer and I are not concerned with politics. Our present business is murder."

"Sounds like one of those thrillers," said Springer, so suddenly and with such a blank expression that Prentice was not sure whether he had really spoken.

"Anyway," he went on, "Robert was in a flap and didn't know what to do. I told him he'd better go out and leave Jenny to cool off. If he stayed out late she'd have to go by half past ten, and things might look better in the morning. He said that was a good idea and that he might look in on the dance at College—it goes on till eleven. After a bit, he went. He seemed a little more cheerful."

"He went to the dance, you say. What time was that?"

"Well, he said he was going. I didn't see him again. It was five to ten."

"What did you do then?"

"I couldn't do any more work. Putting Robert right had taken it out of me. I played Beethoven's Fifth."

"It was on the wireless?"

"No, on my record-player."

"You have a wireless and a record-player. You must be fond of music, Mr. Prentice."

"I don't get out much. I've got to work pretty hard on my research, and after a day in the lab. there's plenty to do in the evening, checking results and catching up on my other reading. I'm not very fond of dances and things like that. And I love music."

"So do I. Beethoven's Fifth takes twenty-nine minutes if it's played at the proper speed. So your record finished about ten-twenty-five. What then?"

As Ludlow had already discovered, one should not underestimate the police in any direction. Prentice swallowed hard with surprise before answering.

"I just sort of sat back, thinking. It must have been about ten minutes later that I heard all the noise upstairs. I thought that Robert must have come back and was having some trouble with Jenny, so I ran up to see. Mr. Latham had just got the door open and—well, there she was. Horrible. I stood around until Mr. Latham came back with the Warden and Mr. Ludlow from the English department. Then he—Mr. Ludlow, started interfering with the scarf round her neck. I told him he ought to leave her alone, and he asked me to get the police. Of course I couldn't argue."

"So it was you who rang the Yard?"

"Yes. Tom—the porter—went out to get Dr. Hastings."

"We must be grateful to you for your prompt action. Just two more questions. Was Miss Hexham in room 27 all the time that Robert Trent was with you?"

"Oh no, I forgot. I asked him if she was there, and he said she'd gone up to talk to her cousin Michael, on the floor above. He'd given her his key to get in, for her coat and things. I suppose he knew she'd hang about the Hall for as long as she could."

"So he had decided to go out before you advised him to do so?"

"I'm not sure if he had. I think he just couldn't take any more and wanted to get away from her on any excuse. Are those your two final questions?"

"No, the last was a kind of supplementary. Just this: did

you hear any kind of disturbance in the room above, between Mr. Trent leaving you and the arrival of Mr. Latham?"

"No, nothing. I had the record on pretty loud. And sound doesn't pass up and down very easily in this building. There's fibre-glass between the floors."

"But you heard the noise when Mr. Latham arrived."

"He was outside the room. Noise travels down the stairs all right."

"Well, thank you, Mr. Prentice. That's been very helpful. We may have a word with you again, but you can go to bed now. I wonder if you'd mind sending along that Polish student who's waiting."

"Steve? Certainly." At the door he hesitated. "I hope I didn't say anything to make you suspect Robert—I mean, his quarrelling with her. He's not the sort to harm anybody, I can assure you of that."

"It's too soon yet for suspicions. You certainly needn't worry about anything you've told us."

"I don't think much of the bunch we've seen so far," said Springer as the door closed behind Prentice. "If this is what they call going to college, give me the old section-house any day. The three older ones upstairs were a proper set of comics too. And that chap Ludlow interfering with the evidence, and then acting daft."

"He's a very intelligent man, Jack."

"So they all ought to be, sir. They're professors, aren't they?"

"It doesn't always follow, unfortunately. Ah, here's our Pole."

A pale young man, looking frightened and defiant at the same time, entered the room and clicked his heels with an accompanying bow. Montero, not to be outdone, rose and motioned him to a chair.

"What is your full name?"

"Stefan Zawadzka. But as you will not be able to pronounce it, you may call me Steve."

"How do you spell that?" asked Springer.

"S-t-e-v-e."

"No, the other one."

Steve told him, while Springer tried to avoid his superior's eye. Montero took up the questioning again.

"Now, this has nothing to do with your evidence, of course. But for the record, I believe you are of Polish nationality?"

"I am Polish, yes."

"How long have you been in this country, Mr. Zawaski —er, Steve?"

"Nearly a year, and I will stay here. Last year, I came over on a visit of students, but I would not go back when the others go. I ask for the political asylum. Poland is in the hands of bad men. My poor country bleeds again."

"Yes, a bad business." Montero was sympathetic. "And you suffered so much in the war."

"So much. Mr. Inspector, you cannot know how much. I was only a little child, but I can remember terrible things. First the Germans came, then the Russians: but you and the Americans—you should never have allowed the Russians to come so far."

"I'm sure you're right, Steve. But I don't know much about these political things. By the way, Jenny Hexham was mixed up with the Communists, wasn't she?"

"She was a big one. Ah, she was a bad woman. It is good that she is dead. That shocks you, yes? One should not hate people, this I know for I am a good Catholic. But I say with all my heart that I hated her. She threatened me, she tried to make me work for them, and said things

29

would happen to my family in Poland if I refused. But I will never work for those swine, never."

"Did you see her alive this evening?" asked Montero in an attempt to get back to the facts of the case.

"Yes, at eight o'clock or so. She was knocking on Robert Trent's door. That poor man, she would not leave him alone. He is a fool, he believes that the Communists wish good. But he is not bad; they deceive him."

"Where were you when you saw her?"

"Just going into my room. It is across from his. I saw him let her in. Mr. Latham came past, up the stairs. I said to him, 'She is bad, that one.' He looked at me strange, and said nothing."

"And what did you do for the rest of the evening?"

"I was reading in my room. Later, I go to the common room to look at the papers. When I came back, the wind has banged my door shut, the key is in my other coat. I say damn. I go to get the special key and open the door again."

"What time was that?"

"About ten o'clock."

"You got the master-key from the porter?"

"Yes. When I open my door, I take the crowd of keys —what do you say——?"

"Bunch," said Montero and Springer together.

"Thank you, yes, the bunch —I give it to the porter, then back to my room.'"

"Did you leave the keys on the porter's desk?"

"I gave them to him."

"To Ferris himself—you're sure of that?"

"But yes, of course."

"Did you stay in your room after that?"

"Yes, until I heard Mr. Latham shouting outside

30

Robert's room, and I come out to see what happens. She is dead. I will pray for her soul, but it is better so."

"Now try to think carefully, Steve. Did you hear anybody go in or out of that room after you came back from leaving your keys?"

"I do not think so. Here there is much noise, so one does not notice very much. They shout, they sing, they run about. In Poland too it is the same. All over the world, the students——"

"You didn't hear anybody go in or out of that room, not to be sure?"

"No."

"I think that's all for now. We'll probably see you again."

After Steve had clicked and bowed himself out, Montero and Springer looked at each other.

"Well, there's one good lie from somebody, sir," said Springer. "Either that chap or the porter's telling lies about the keys."

"Yes. And we've got something else that may be useful. He said that Latham saw the girl coming in, and seemed to react a bit strangely. Latham was in a terrible state of nerves all the time we were with him."

"I suppose it's natural, sir. People like that aren't as used to this sort of thing as we are. It must be a bit off-putting to find a body."

"Surely. But I think there's more to it than that. We'd better have another talk with Latham before we go. Who else is there waiting?"

"The cousin, Michael Hexham. Shall I fetch him, sir? There are one or two others who just seem to have drifted up to the room later on."

"Yes, we'll have Hexham. You go along quietly to

fetch him—and see if Steve what's-'is-name has gone back to that room. That's why I didn't ask him to do it."

"You think they're in something together, sir?"

"I think Steve must know more than he's said. Either he's in it with Ferris and they've got their stories mixed up or else—well, as I said, it's too early for suspects yet. Give me a nod when you come back, if you've spotted anything."

But Springer only shook his head when he returned with Michael Hexham. There are many students who feel contempt for the forces of authority in general and their own tutors in particular, but not all of them show it. Hexham was one of those who show it plainly. He was a rather small, dark youth, with thin lips and a tendency towards a moustache. His usual face was one of amused superiority. When shaken out of his complacency, as he now was, he became childishly cantankerous. Montero found no difficulty in dealing with him.

"I won't keep you long, Mr. Hexham. This must have been a terrible shock for you."

"Frightful. I don't say she didn't deserve it, but it's quite knocked me over."

"Do I take it that you disapproved of your cousin's activities?"

"Well, naturally, I mean all this Communist stuff. And then the way she behaved generally. I'd warned her about it many times, but she always laughed. Though I wouldn't have expected Robert Trent to be the one to do it."

"You think that Mr. Trent murdered her?"

"It's pretty obvious, isn't it? She'd been in his room all the evening. Then she's found there dead, and he's disappeared."

"Well, we mustn't jump to conclusions. But how did you know she had been there earlier in the evening?"

"She came to my room. I suppose Robert couldn't stand any more of her, and cleared out. She was always coming to me to gloat over what she'd done. She knew I had to listen and keep quiet about it."

"Was she gloating this evening?"

"Well no, she talked quite sensibly. She was rather quiet, for her. But she seemed happy, so she'd probably been up to something."

"What time did she come to you?"

"About a quarter past nine."

"Did she stay long?"

"Over an hour. At last I told her she'd have to go by half past ten, so she went to see if Robert had come back."

"Had he gone out, then?"

"I don't know whether he'd left the building—she didn't say."

"If she had his key, how was he going to get back into his room after she'd gone?"

"I suppose she'd have left it in the door, outside. We quite often do that, if we want to borrow something from each other."

"Not very safe, is it?"

"Nothing ever happens."

"It has now. However. Now your room, I think, is on the floor above room 27—the same floor as Mr. Latham?"

"Yes. I'm immediately above Robert. Mr. Latham is on the other side of the corridor."

"Did you hear any unusual sounds from below you during the evening?"

"No. Sound doesn't travel much from floor to floor in this building."

"I know—there's fibre-glass between the floors. But you heard enough to make you go down when the body was discovered."

"I heard Tom come up to Mr. Latham, and I heard a lot of running about and shouting. You couldn't miss that."

"Did you come down immediately?"

"Only after the noise had gone on for a time. I got there just after the Warden, I think."

"Mr. Hexham, you said just now that your cousin knew you had to listen to her and say nothing. Would you mind telling me what you meant?"

"I don't think I said that."

Springer read without expression, "'She knew I had to listen and keep quiet.'"

"It's a bit off, taking down what a man says. You haven't given me the usual warning, that it will be used in evidence against me."

"We never do say that: only that it 'may be used in evidence.' This won't be. If formal evidence is required from you, you'll have to give it. This is just a preliminary inquiry."

"I don't see what family affairs can have to do with this murder—because it is that, isn't it?" Michael seemed relieved to have spoken the word.

"It is murder, and I'd hoped you would help us to solve it. If you don't want to, I can't compel you to say anything."

"Of course I want it solved. The point was simply that Jenny's family didn't know about her belonging to the Communists."

"That's your family too?"

"Her father and mine are brothers. It's mainly our

34

grandmother I'm worried about. She's been very good to both of us. It might kill her to know the truth about Jenny —her heart isn't strong and she mustn't have any shock. This business will probably finish her. Jenny was always threatening to let it all out."

"Why should she want to kill her grandmother?"

"I didn't say that. You keep twisting my words. Still, she did stand to gain from it. Grandmother's money is coming to both of us, divided equally."

"Much money?"

"About fifty thousand, I think."

"And now you are the sole legatee?"

"I suppose so. All right, I strangled Jenny so that Grandmother would die of the shock and I'd get all her money. Now go on—arrest me—that's what you've been working up to all the time."

Montero sighed deeply and rose. "Mr. Hexham," he said, "you are upset and overtired. Go to bed, and stop making it difficult for us." Michael looked deflated and went to the door like a rebellious schoolboy. Montero stopped him before he could open it.

"One more question, if you can bear it. Did your cousin have her handbag with her while she was in your room?"

"I don't think so. No, she didn't. I remember her putting the key to Robert's room on the arm of her chair."

"She took it with her when she left?"

"Yes." Michael went without waiting for any more questions. Montero and Springer looked at each other without enthusiasm.

"That young man's a poor witness," said Montero, "but I think we can make sense of what we've got so far only by assuming that he's telling the truth. Let's have another word with Latham and then push off. First, you'd better check that there's no news of Trent. I sent Perks round to have a look for him."

There was neither news nor rumour. Detective-Constable Perkins had been to every room in the Hall. After this considerable feat, he was set to guard Trent's room, with promise of a relief later. Sergeant Macalister, who had been working on fingerprints, was gloomy when Montero spoke to him.

"The room's full of them, sir," he said. "So smudged and mixed up that I don't expect we can get much sense out of them. I'll do my best, but I reckon these boys are in and out of each other's rooms all the time. Did you notice that chair though—the one that was lying on its side?"

"I didn't look closely at it. Was there a good print on it?"

"No, sir, but I did notice that there were scratches on the top of the back—just faint ones where the varnish had been scraped off. I don't know if it means anything."

"Good work to notice it anyway. We'll have another look later."

When Montero eventually called on Latham again, he was prepared to apologise for keeping him out of bed. Latham, however, was fully dressed and sitting up by an ashtray full of cigarette ends, looking as if he had been there without moving for a considerable time.

"I'm sorry to bother you again, sir," said Montero, "but I'd just like to ask you a few things that might help us in our inquiries. General things mostly, about the way this place is run. Now first, have all the young men here got separate rooms, with their own keys?"

"They usually share a room in their first year and then have a single one. They all have Yale locks and keys—the

36

rooms, I mean." Latham seemed to be glad of a chance to talk.

"Suppose one of them leaves the key in his room and then shuts the door on himself—does that ever happen?"

"They're always doing it. Then they get a key from the porter on duty."

"A duplicate of their own key, or a master?"

"There's a master-key for each floor. I think the porter keeps them all on a bunch, with cleaners' cupboard keys and so on."

"So anybody can get at all the master-keys at any time?"

"I suppose so: if the porter's there to give them to him."

"Has anybody else got master-keys?"

"I have them, for the rooms in this block. The Warden has a complete set."

"I see. Thank you. Now, the front door is locked at ten and guests must leave then, or by ten-thirty on Saturdays. The students cannot leave the building after ten, but can stay out till midnight. Have I got all that right?"

"Yes."

"Is there anything to stop one of them letting himself out after ten, or doing the same for a guest?"

"The front door has a lock that can be opened only from inside. The porter keeps the key—and of course the Warden and I have one."

"But I dare say the students have other ways of getting in and out?"

"Occasionally. Of course, they're expelled if they're caught."

"When you went to Mr. Trent's room this evening, had you any reason to expect to find him there?"

"Only that the porter said he hadn't gone out. I knew nothing about it."

"Well, thank you, Mr. Latham. I expect you want to get to bed. Quarter to one. Come on, Springheels, we'll have to make an early start tomorrow."

"Lovely idea for a Sunday morning," said Springer.

"You shouldn't have joined."

As they stepped out on the landing, a terrifying scream came from somewhere below. It was followed by a thud and a burst of maniacal laughter. Montero hurried towards the stairs.

"That's nothing," said Latham cheerfully, "just Saturday night."

"Don't they ever go to bed?"

"I don't think some of them ever do."

They went downstairs, stopping on the way to speak to Perkins. Tom Ferris was standing in the entrance hall.

"You're off then, Inspector," he said.

"Yes. Before we go—are you quite sure that the keys that were borrowed were left on your desk in your absence, and not given to you?"

"That's right."

"The whole bunch?"

"Yes. But I noticed something after I'd talked to you. There's one missing—the one that fits the rooms on the second floor where that girl was killed."

CHAPTER III

The students were not the only ones who were acting on the belief that to be out of bed after midnight is to be up betimes. When Ludlow had said good-night to Blake, he wandered back to the block where the murder had taken place. On the first floor, he saw Henry Prentice going into his room.

"I'm glad you haven't gone, sir," said Prentice. "I thought of coming over to see if you were still with the Warden. I wanted to apologise for how I spoke to you upstairs."

"That's all right," said Ludlow.

"I just thought it would be better to leave it to the police."

"No doubt your social instincts are quite correct, and show an excellent training in civics and jurisprudence. I commend them, but I am old-fashioned enough to believe that the possibility of saving life should come first. But let it pass—I did no good and probably no harm. Are you a budding lawyer?"

"No, sir. A chemist."

"Are you a friend of Robert Trent's?" Ludlow asked the question unexpectedly and with a force that was quite unlike his usual manner.

"We get on pretty well."

"Have you seen him this evening?"

Prentice hesitated. "I've made a statement to the police,

Mr. Ludlow. I'm not sure if I ought to talk to other people while they're investigating."

"Look, Prentice, I'll ask you one question, and your answer to that will decide whether you want to tell me any more. Do you think that Trent murdered Jenny Hexham?"

"Not from what I know of him. No, I don't."

"Nor do I. But a lot of people are going to think so. I don't want to see one of my best honours men wasting time in a police station, and possibly in a criminal court. If you can tell me anything, it might help me to help him."

Prentice was silent for a moment. Then he held his door open and invited Ludlow to come in. Their conversation was much the same as the one Prentice had already had with Montero.

"Well, you've given me some ideas anyway, and I'm grateful to you," said Ludlow. "If Robert was upset when he came to you, he may have reasons of his own for running away. It's a pity you don't know anything about that last thirty minutes. But you didn't leave your room all that time?"

"No, sir. I listened to the symphony straight through and didn't get up until I heard the voices upstairs."

"Nothing happened to interrupt you?"

"No. I remember thinking how quiet it was for a Saturday, and how pleasant to be able to hear a record through without any disturbance."

"Thank you." Ludlow got up. "You've no idea where Robert might have gone."

"I'm afraid not."

Leaving Prentice's room, Ludlow nearly fell over a small, untidy figure carrying a saucepan. Disentangling himself from Ludlow's long legs, the student gave a broad grin of recognition.

"Hullo, sir. Like some coffee?"

Ludlow recognised one of his first-year students who, as he often remarked, put more energy into making excuses for not having done essays than would have been needed to do them. This young man, Pratt by name, shared a room with an equally tousled urchin who was a potential physicist called Huggett. They looked remarkably alike and lived in a happy squalor that was the despair of Blake.

"No, thank you," said Ludlow. "I no longer find that coffee acts as a soporific, though you young men seem to be able to sleep after it. But I'll come in and talk to you while you drink it, if I may."

He went in, and a place was cleared for him to sit on one of the two tousled beds in the room.

"It's rather exciting, isn't it," said Pratt, "having a murder here? The Warden always says he doesn't know what's going to happen next. Fancy Bob Trent doing her in."

"I don't think he did, which is why I'm still here at this ghastly hour," said Ludlow. "Were you two here all the evening?"

"Yes—we didn't go to the dance at college. They're square. The medical schools are the best for getting really hep, but we decided it wasn't worth going in the rain."

"So you stayed in, and read *Beowulf* and split an atom or two?"

"Well, we stayed in. We just nattered, and sat around."

"All the evening?"

"Yes. It's surprising how the time goes when you're talking," said Huggett with the air of one who had made an important discovery.

"I've noticed that myself. So nothing exciting happened?"

"No. He must have been finishing her off while we were here. I wish I'd gone upstairs and seen him," said Pratt.

"I wish you had, too. It would have saved a lot of trouble. You didn't go out of this room at all?"

"No. Well—only to mend the fuse."

Both students suddenly became uncomfortable and looked at each other, then at Ludlow, then at the electric ring on which the coffee was beginning to boil.

"I see. You fused the lights with that device?"

"You won't tell the Warden, will you, sir? We're not supposed to have these things really, but it saves money on the gas and it's jolly useful for boiling things. We had it on for a few minutes to warm up the room, and it blew the fuse."

"It's the wattage," said Huggett knowingly, "it's too much for this circuit."

"Won't it blow again now?" asked Ludlow.

Huggett looked proud. "I've fixed that all right. Put in a good strong piece of steel wire. We won't have any more trouble tonight."

"What time did this happen?" asked Ludlow, praying for protection from fire.

"Quarter past ten. The lights were only out for two or three minutes and nobody complained. In fact, the place seemed pretty dead."

"An unfortunate metaphor, Pratt. I'd like to ask you something else. I don't suppose either of you would leave this building after hours, but let us suppose as a point of academic discussion that you found yourselves with the front door locked and a great need to get into the street. What would you do?"

"Slip out the back way into the courtyard, and climb the wall into the street at the side," Huggett said without hesitation. "It's quite easy."

"Or there's the way through the boiler-house," said Pratt. "Down the basement steps, and you crawl over the coke and up through the chute into the street."

"It mucks up your clothes," said Huggett, though neither of the two looked as if a trip across the coke would make much difference to his appearance.

"Well, thanks for your hospitality. If you think of anything else about this evening, perhaps you'll let me know."

Ludlow decided to go before he received any more awful revelations about the ways of Mudge Hall. His wanderings about the building led him next to have a word with Steve, who was very willing to talk and repeated what he had told Montero. Then Ludlow, in spite of the late hour, climbed another flight of stairs to talk to Michael Hexham. His interview with Montero had deflated Hexham enough to make him fairly civil and co-operative until he was asked:

"Why did you call out that your cousin's bracelet had been stolen?"

"It was missing. Obviously the murderer had taken it."

"I'm surprised that you should notice it had gone, at a time like that!"

"She always wore it, on her right wrist. It was very conspicuous—a wide, heavy piece of pure gold."

"It must be very valuable."

"It is. It's a sort of heirloom. My grandmother gave it to her on her birthday two years ago."

"The grandmother from whom you have—expectations?"

"Yes, if you put it like that."

"I wonder if you could give me the address where your cousin was lodging in London."

"Why do you want it?"

"Because," said Ludlow, keeping his temper with difficulty, "I want to help Robert Trent. That is my only concern, and the way to do it is to find the real murderer. If you don't want to co-operate, I'm acting as a private person and I can put no pressure on you. I can find out the address from the College office, but that means waiting until Monday. If I can follow it up tomorrow, there may be something to be learnt."

Hexham gave the address, and Ludlow wished him good-night. On the way out, he talked to Tom Ferris, whose loquacity was a welcome change from the difficulty of getting anything out of Hexham.

"By the way," said Ludlow as he was leaving, "you might have a look at the fuse-box on the first floor. I think you'll find a piece of steel wire in one of the fuses." Ferris swore lengthily about "them students" and their habits with electrical appliances.

"They'll have us all burned to death one night," he said. "Then I'll be the one to get the blame. It's an unjust world."

"And virtue is triumphant only in theatrical performances," said Ludlow; but Ferris did not know his Gilbert and Sullivan and he looked sulky as he let Ludlow out.

Next morning saw Ludlow in his old Austin called Cleopatra—because, as he said, Age cannot wither her, nor custom stale her infinite variety—driving through the deserted streets. To a real Londoner, there are few sights more pleasant than Oxford Street on a Sunday morning when it is possible to see one's way ahead and to move on foot or in a car without mortal peril. The storm had blown itself out and the sun was shining. Ludlow felt cheerful in spite of his errand, and allowed himself a little honest excitement. It is agreeable to linger on the fringe of other people's crimes and remain untouched by them, a fact that the psychologists can explain in what dark ways they please. He rattled away down the Bayswater Road, where Jamaicans stood about to praise the late autumnal sun, drove through the avenue of almost leafless trees at Holland Park and came to the howling wastes of Uxbridge Road. Such are the problems of living in London that students who are not in hostels often find themselves a very long way from their colleges.

Though Jenny Hexham need not have chosen quite such a seedy area, Ludlow thought as he passed Shepherd's Bush station and turned off into even shabbier streets. Houses that had once been highly respectable, although never fashionable, now bulged out their unpainted façades like decayed and uncorseted dowagers. Ludlow found the number that he was looking for; the railings, long ago removed to make part of a cruiser, had never been replaced and the basement area gaped ravenously behind a twist of wire. He climbed grimy steps, pressed the bell and waited. After five minutes and two further attempts it dawned on his scientific mind that the bell was out of order. The heavy iron knocker produced better results: a small shriek and a retreating patter of slippered feet. A grey, untidy head came out of a first-floor window.

"Well?" it demanded.

"Good morning, madam. I wonder if I could see you for a few minutes?"

"If it's about that girl, I'm telling nobody nothing else,

and it's no good you saying you're the police because I've been had that way once already this morning."

"I am certainly not the police. But I have an interest in this matter."

"You a private detective?"

"Well," said Ludlow thoughtfully, "yes, I suppose you might say I am." The idea pleased him and did not seem too far beyond the truth. He opened his wallet, took out a pound note and looked at it thoughtfully. The head reacted.

"Wait," it said, "I'll be down."

The door soon opened and the head appeared attached to a body in a brown garment that might have been either a dressing-gown or an overall. The pound note vanished into one of its recesses.

"I'll tell you what I told the police, and no more. There was a man here at nine o'clock—nine, I ask you, on a Sunday—said Miss Hexham wouldn't be coming back and could he get some of her things for her. No, he couldn't, I said. And she's paid a week's rent and nobody's taking nothing. He showed me her keys, said she sent him to collect some things. But I wouldn't budge—then he says he's from the police. I asked for his card—I know a thing or two, I've seen the police here before. That sent him off quick with a flea in his ear."

She paused triumphantly for breath. Ludlow wondered whether he was going to hear any more for a pound.

"Thank you, Mrs.—er——"

"Reddle, dear—though Reddle's been gone these six months."

"I'm so sorry."

"He'll be back though, like the bad penny he is."

"He's not dead then?"

46

"Dead? Bless your heart, no. He's inside—over there."

She gestured northwards towards Wormwood Scrubs. Ludlow struggled to bring the conversation back.

"This man who came this morning—could you describe him? Would you know him again?"

"Know him anywhere. He was big, not as tall as you, dear, but fatter." She looked affectionately at Ludlow as if she would like to start fattening him. "He had a fawn raincoat and a trilby hat, and he had a big black beard and moustache—covered half his face. And he wore dark glasses; must have had bad eyes."

Ludlow slowly counted to twenty before thanking her.

"And the real police came later?"

"Soon as he'd left, almost. They were here, poking about all over the place. Only went ten minutes before you came."

"You couldn't tell me any more about the first man? What was his voice like?"

"He had a gruff, hoarse sort of voice. Didn't open his lips much. And I did notice he was a very heavy smoker; his fingers were quite brown."

Ludlow thanked her again and retreated down the steps to the accompaniment of Mrs. Reddle's voice, now fully loosened.

"I always thought that girl would come to no good. Out to all hours, though I always give my lodgers perfect freedom to come and go as they like. Fancy her murdered though—some of them students must be a bad lot. That's a nice car, dear—got character——"

Cleopatra responded with a roar, and Ludlow drove off. He was deep in one of his moods of self-reproach.

There you are, he said to himself, failed again. Too late. If you'd only got up early you'd have been there before any of them and caught the murderer. He was quite cheerful by the time he turned back into the Uxbridge Road.

CHAPTER IV

Fresh from their encounter with Mrs. Reddle, Montero and Springer were by this time back at Mudge Hall, having a conference in the study-room which had been set aside for them.

"I hate this sort of case, sir," said Springer mournfully. "When we've got a lot of statements, some of them obviously lies, and nothing definite to go on. And all the work in front of us."

"Never mind, Springheels—it's what the taxpayer provides a pittance for us to do. When you've been at this game as long as I have, you'll know the value of all those dull statements. It isn't the sensational crimes that take the work—they usually lead straight to one person. This is our bread and butter—a killing that several people had reason and opportunity for. And we've got to find who it is. And you know how to get me talking and wasting time, don't you?"

Springer grinned. "It seems to me, sir," he said, "that we've only got one chap to find, and he's hopped it."

"You're plumping for young Trent, are you?"

"It seems pretty clear to me."

"Well, let's look at what we've got so far. Take the undisputed facts first and go from there. Jenny Hexham entered this building at eight—seen by three people—and went to Robert Trent's room. At nine-fifteen she and Trent came out of that room and separated. He went down to the next floor to talk to Prentice, stayed with him for about forty-five minutes and then said that he was going out. She was with her cousin, Michael Hexham, until nearly half past ten, when she went back to Trent's room to which she had the key. At ten-forty, Latham and the porter got into the room and found her dead. The window was wide open, the fire-escape had been used to let somebody down into the courtyard. Right?"

"Excuse me, sir, if Hexham is lying a lot of that falls down."

"Quite. But let's assume he's telling the truth, and see where it gets us. Let's suppose that Trent didn't leave the house, but went back to his room to wait for Jenny. After ten, he couldn't have got out by the front door, so it would have been he who used the fire-escape. But he may have gone out, as he said he was going to, so somebody else got into his room—the murderer. Now, who could have opened his door?"

"Shall we make a list, sir?"

"Yes. First, the Warden apparently has keys to the whole house. Unless he and this chap Ludlow are in a deep plot together, he didn't leave his own quarters all the evening. Also, no apparent motive. Latham, the Sub-Warden, has keys to this block. No known motive, but note that he was apparently agitated when he saw the girl arrive and went to pieces later."

"If he did it, he'd have had to be quick to get down the fire-escape and back to his room, and be sitting there when the porter came."

"Fair enough. We'll keep him on the list, but without enthusiasm."

"Then there's the porter, Ferris. I didn't like the look of him very much."

"Nor did I, but if I arrested everybody who came in that category I'd soon depopulate London. Ferris had access to the keys and could go almost anywhere in the building without suspicion. Apparently no motive, though he says himself that he took a dim view of the girl and her activities. He was in a position to know who came and went. If Trent did in fact go out just before the door was locked at ten, Ferris would have known that she was still here and could have waited for her. Then there's Steve, the Pole we can't pronounce, who was known to have had the key to rooms on that floor during the evening. He hated the girl for her Communism, and she was apparently threatening him through his family. Now note this very carefully—either he or Ferris is lying about the return of the keys."

"Suppose Ferris is telling the truth, sir. If the keys were left out on the desk, anybody could have got at them."

"I know. The question is whether that particular key was removed from the bunch before or after Steve brought them back. And why did he lie about what he did with them?"

"Perhaps he thought that he'd get into trouble for leaving them lying around."

"Maybe. Now next we've got Michael Hexham, on whose word alone we have to rely for Jenny's movements after nine-fifteen. Nothing to stop him from going back to the room with her, killing her there and escaping. He has a fair motive in the prospect of doubling, and perhaps speeding up, a very substantial legacy. Also dislike of her activities, for family reasons. Finally we have your favourite in this race——"

"Robert Trent, sir."

"Now he, if he never left the building, could have gone

back to his room, waited for Jenny to return and killed her, and then got out of the window when he was alarmed by Latham at the door."

"How did he get back, if he'd given her the key?"

"Exactly. And why did he give it her and let her go out and talk to her cousin, if he had it in his mind to kill her? Have I shaken your faith a little?"

"I see what you mean, sir. But if he's innocent, why did he run away?"

"When we find him, we shall know. His description's been circulated. He certainly seems to have had a good motive."

"Is that the lot, sir?"

"For the moment. Though if Ferris is telling the truth about the keys, anybody in the building might be under suspicion. Anybody could have picked the keys up and taken the one he wanted, while they were lying on the desk. But I've a feeling we shan't have to look much farther than the little group we've got our eyes on."

"There are two other possibilities, sir."

"I know, but I don't think much of them. Still, let's have them."

"She could have let anybody in after she went back to the room, or if she left the key somebody could have followed her in. Or the murderer could just have knocked and been let in by her."

"Right. But I think the chap was waiting for her. He could hang about to see when the coast was clear. If he had to go in with her or just after, somebody might have come along and seen him. Besides, if Hexham is telling the truth, she went just before ten-thirty. Somebody who knew his way about the building, and the rules, would have known she had to go back to the room for her things.

I'm pretty certain he waited in there for her. It gave him the advantage of surprise too."

"Then Trent could have given her his key as a blind, got the master-key and gone back to wait for her after giving everybody the idea that he'd left the building?"

"Yes, he could. Now what's our other possibility?"

"Whoever was waiting for her—and I'm sure you're right that it was done that way—could have forced the lock. This type is easy to open."

"Don't we know it! A table knife will do it, but it's likely to leave marks, and there were none here. Also it takes just long enough to be risky in a place like this where there are people about all the time. I doubt whether anybody in this Hall knows the celluloid trick, and even that takes a moment or two. No, I think if we can find who took that master-key off the bunch, we shall have our man."

"It might have been somebody from outside, sir, one of her queer friends."

"Could be. But the porter was in the Hall all the evening, except from eight to eight-thirty when Trent and the girl were together in the room. The second time that Ferris went away, the door had been locked."

"If he's telling the truth."

"Every sentence begins with *if* in this sort of case. I think the room was entered, with a master-key, by someone who knew his way about the Hall, but I could be wrong. Let's leave it at that for the moment and look at the other stuff—doctor's report and the rest. Our man's looked at her by now, I suppose?"

"I've got the report here, sir. She was killed by strangulation with a ligature—presumably the scarf that fellow cut off her neck. Great force was used, causing internal injuries to the throat as well as asphyxia. The murderer probably came behind her and seized the ends of her scarf."

"So either he took her completely by surprise when she came back to the room, or he was somebody she knew and trusted. Time of death?"

"About ten-thirty."

"Yes, we could have told him that. Now what about the room itself—prints and other clues?"

"Several recent prints, but we haven't been able to check on them—apart from her own of course. None of them are in the record, anyway. There are three sets on the door-handle, but they've messed each other up so much that I doubt if we can get a clear identification. One seems to be hers, as we'd expect. One is probably Latham's."

"And the other, if we can disentangle it, is the murderer's. Not much hope there, I'm afraid. Anything else?"

"Nothing much, sir. The room showed no sign of struggle. There's that chair on the floor; scratches on the top rung of the back, caused recently, probably by some metal object. Her coat was in the room; it might have been gone through by the murderer, or it might just have been thrown down carelessly in the first place. Her handbag was lying open, with its contents scattered about. Until we know what was in it first, we can't tell what was taken. Her purse had about two pounds in it."

Montero stretched out his hand for the report and studied it for a moment.

"One interesting omission from the things found in her bag, but we'll come to that later," he said. "These scratches on her right wrist may be important; if she was trying to defend herself and he pulled her hand away, *he* may have scratches on his own wrist—or on his face. Now the next thing is to check on all her known associates. If we believe all we've been told so far, she was a pretty regrettable character—a known Communist and not above a bit of blackmail for the Party."

"She seems to have been something of a loose woman too," said Springer with such a surprisingly old-fashioned primness that Montero might have laughed if he had not known his subordinate's ways well.

"Quite so. In fact, there are probably quite a lot of people who are glad she's dead—and one of them glad enough to be the one who killed her. Now what have we learnt this morning? A man, obviously disguised in a crude, impromptu way, has been to her lodgings and asked to go through her things. He claimed to be in possession of her keys. That's the significant omission from the things in her bag—no keys. In fact this whole case is becoming a question of keys."

"You mean, sir, that the murderer stole her keys last night? Was it necessary to murder her to get them?"

"I don't suppose that was the motive for the murder, only one of its results. He wanted something that she'd got. Maybe he killed her when she refused to give it him. Whatever it was, he thought it might be at her lodgings and tried to get in first and find it."

"We didn't find anything there worth doing a murder for, sir."

"Have you ever heard what Sherlock Holmes said about the dog in the night?"

"No, but I'll buy it."

"You needn't look so eager, it's not a dirty one. The remarkable thing was that the dog did nothing in the night. The remarkable thing about our search this morning is that it yielded no evidence of the sort of girl she was. From her things, she might have been just an ordinary well-behaved student. No Communist publications, no incriminating letters, either political or personal. Yet she was in possession of some documents that could frighten people. Where are they? We don't know, and the chap who called at her lodgings doesn't know. He took a risk, by the way—must have known we'd be round there pretty soon. I suppose I ought to have put a man there last night, we haven't got all those to spare."

"If we'd got there ten minutes earlier this morning, we'd have grabbed the murderer without any trouble."

"Not necessarily. We'd have grabbed someone who knows more about this business than is good for him, but it might be an accomplice. All we know about him is that he's big and apparently a heavy smoker. We might check on that, by the way."

"I did, sir, while you were having another look at the room after we got back. I had a word with one or two people. Of those we interviewed last night, Ferris and Latham are fairly heavy smokers, Hexham smokes very occasionally. The others don't at all—and that includes Trent."

"I looked for cigarettes when I was going over his room again. Anyway, his description makes him out much smaller than our disguised friend."

"Do we take Trent off the list then?"

"By no means. It's quite on the cards that he passed the keys to somebody while he lies low. If that's so, it makes the whole affair and its motivation a great deal more complicated. Anyway, we've got the house under supervision now, but it's probably too late."

At this moment Ferris put his head round the door, said

sulkily, "Telephone in the hall for Inspector Montero", and withdrew. When Montero came back, he looked thoughtful.

"This is interesting," he said. "A few minutes after we left that lodging-house, a man arrived in an old car and had a conversation with Mrs. Reddle, during which he was seen to give her money. His description sounds exactly like Ludlow. Our man got the number of his car, so we can soon check that. I think we'll be having another word with Mr. Ludlow."

Ludlow meanwhile was having another word with Michael Hexham, happily unconscious that a few yards away his description was being sent from one policeman to another. Like most of the students in Mudge Hall, Michael regarded Sunday morning as a time for staying in bed, and his resentment at being got up was added to his natural sulkiness. Ludlow was working hard on him.

"Look here," he said at last, "you seem to think that I have some sinister interest in all this. I don't care twopence about you, and I must admit that I don't care about your family either. All I want to do is to find Robert Trent, an extremely good student who's likely to come to some kind of harm if I don't get hold of him soon. If I do find him, we are probably a long way towards finding the murderer —and that's where your interest comes in."

"I don't see that," said Michael. "What good will it do now? It's no good pretending that I'm burning for revenge or anything like that. I'm sorry about Jenny, but we didn't get on, and there it is."

"There it is. So plainly that you are under grave suspicion of having murdered her."

"That's ridiculous."

"I had a long talk with Inspector Montero last night," said Ludlow, wondering how far he could get without telling an open lie, "and I've learnt some more facts this morning."

Michael swallowed hard and reached for a cigarette. Ludlow pressed his advantage.

"Surely you'd be glad to see the real murderer brought to justice," he said with a silent groan at the necessary cliché.

Michael reverted to his usual supercilious manner. "Suppose it turns out to be Robert Trent?" he said.

"Then I'm proved wrong and you're cleared, so you can have a double laugh."

"But what makes you think you can do better than the police?"

Ludlow took a moment to reflect how adequately he could put this young man in his place if so much did not depend on his co-operation.

"Because I know Robert, and they don't. I've taught him for over two years and I think I have some influence with him. He's run away because he's afraid of being suspected of killing your cousin. It may be that he knows things that would put his own life in danger. The more people who are looking for him the better, especially if one of them happens to be a man whom he trusts."

Michael appeared to think this over, and to decide that his own interest was in fact involved. He said at last, "What do you want to know from me?"

"All you can tell me about your cousin's activities, particularly places where she used to go to meet her Communist friends. If there are politics in this—and I think there are—Robert may be foolish enough to think he'd be safe with her old associates, even though he was trying to break himself free from them."

"Then I can't help you much. I didn't approve of her activities, and she didn't talk to me about them—only in a general way, to make me feel uncomfortable."

At the thought of Michael being made to feel uncomfortable, Ludlow had a pleasanter mental image of the dead girl.

"Don't you know any of the places she used to go?"

"No—didn't want to be mixed up in anything she did. Well—there was one place—a bookshop near King's Cross that seemed to be a meeting-place for them. I went with her once—she fooled me by saying she was going to browse round a good bookshop she'd discovered. It was a wet afternoon, so I went along, but it was obvious what sort of place it was."

"All Communist books?"

"No, the shop itself seemed genuine enough—I suppose it was a cover. But the man who owned it talked to her about Communism all the time—they were arranging some kind of meeting."

"Where were they going to meet?"

"I didn't take any notice. It was some little café, near the shop—they talked as if they often used it."

"What's the name of the bookshop?"

"I don't know. She kept calling the man Hugh. I just went there with her, and I got so fed up that I came away. I know it was a street behind King's Cross—a grubby little street, off another street that opens into Pentonville Road."

Ludlow decided that he had better be content with these rough directions. He had other questions to ask and did not yet want to arouse Hexham's antagonism. Although he had the authority of his position in the College behind him, he knew that he was crossing rather dangerous ground in taking a murder investigation upon himself. He went on, trying to look more benevolent than he felt:

"Do you know of any enemies your cousin may have had—either in the College or outside?"

Michael Hexham shrugged his shoulders. "Lots, I should think," he said. "It doesn't exactly make one popular with most people in this country to be a known Communist. I know that she used to put pressure on people quite unscrupulously. I mean, once they'd committed themselves at all by going to a Communist meeting or anything like that, she'd threaten to expose it unless they got in deeper."

"Would that be a very strong threat? After all, Communism is not illegal in this country."

"No, but it goes down badly with employers, especially if you want to do any kind of Government or official work. And the more she made out that they were in danger, the more they seemed to be prepared to do."

"Yes, it's the martyr-complex. The worst mistake we could make would be to ban Communism altogether and make it seem heroic to join. But surely some of her—er —victims rebelled."

"You bet they did. Robert for one was trying to pull out. And Steve hated her guts because he was scared what might happen to his family in Poland. Those are the two I happen to know, but there must have been plenty of others."

"Where did she keep all the evidence that frightened people so much? There must have been some kind of documents, more than she would want to carry about with her."

"I don't know where she kept it. She had plenty of stuff certainly—things about the Party, letters people had written. I think she had letters about various affairs she had had. She used to joke about it—said she kept anything that might come in useful. But she didn't keep them with her, nor in her digs. I don't know where, except that it was something only she could get at."

"A safe-deposit in a bank or something like that?"

"Perhaps. She never told anybody. But the secret, whatever it was, was hidden in her bracelet."

Ludlow sat up. "The gold one that was stolen—the one your grandmother gave her?"

Hexham nodded. "That's why I noticed at once that it had been stolen when I first saw her body."

"How did she come to tell you about it?"

"It was at a party that we had—here, in the Hall. She was a bit tight and was showing off about the power she had over people. It was Robert Trent she was going at mostly—making him do little things for her and teasing him. I didn't think anything of it at first, but he got more and more annoyed and at last burst out that she couldn't frighten him without proper evidence, or something like that. She smiled, and then she said that she had plenty of evidence when the time came to use it. Somebody asked her where she kept it. She laughed and said, 'You'd find it if you got to the return of the bracelet that cast so much doubt on a certain person's character.' That was her way of talking—she liked riddles. I suppose she was quite a clever girl really." Hexham paused and looked thoughtful, as people do on discovering a new truth about someone they think they know very well.

"Did this bracelet that has been stolen cast doubt on your cousin's character?" Ludlow asked.

"Well—there was a bit of a row about it. My sister thought it ought to have come to her, because she's the eldest grandchild, and she rather accused Jenny of playing up to Grandmother and trying to get money out of her before she was dead."

"Your sister doesn't come in for any of the legacy?"

"Only a little bit. She's married to quite a rich chap, and Grandmother seems to think she's all right. Jenny was always her favourite."

"How long ago was this party?"

"Oh, about a week—yes, it was last Saturday, a week yesterday."

"This may be very important. Can you remember who was near enough to your cousin to hear what she said about the bracelet?"

"Most of the men in this block were there. It was one of those parties, you know, when several rooms get together and invite girls in, and so on. Robert was with her of course, and Steve, and Jack Febber, and Henry Prentice, and Tony Bates—they were all standing around somewhere near but I don't know if they were listening to her. Oh, and Mr. Latham had dropped in for a drink, and he was with us in that corner."

"Obviously she couldn't have concealed the evidence of a lot of documents under a bracelet, even a very wide one as you say hers was. It looks as if she kept something there that would lead to the papers that a lot of people did not want to be made public. Was that the impression you got from her talking?"

"It was the only thing that seemed to make sense."

"Thank you very much." Ludlow got up. "You've told me something most useful. Did you tell all this to the police last night?"

"No. They didn't ask me."

"Perhaps you ought to." Ludlow went away.

During this private investigation, the more official proceedings had also developed. Montero and Springer had just left their room when they were stopped by a small, dark Indian student, who spoke so quickly that at first they looked blankly at him. On his repeating his question, they understood him to say, "Please, sirs, have you found Robert?"

"If you mean Robert Trent," said Montero, "no we haven't. But we will. May I ask what is your interest in the matter?"

"Robert is a nice boy. I am sorry he should be in this trouble. Last night he said nothing of it to me, and I am sad that he should not trust me. But I hope he will soon come back."

"You saw him last night? At what time?"

"It was nearly half past ten when I saw him last."

The two detectives suddenly came to life. "Now let me get this right," Montero said. "You say you were with Robert Trent until ten-thirty last night?"

"Yes, please. At ten o'clock, I was going through the entrance hall, a bit sad because it was raining so much and there was nobody to talk with. Then Robert was coming in from the back——"

"Excuse my interrupting you, but we must get this quite clear. Do you mean that he came from the courtyard at the back of this building?"

"Yes, there are stairs that go down to the back part. He came in and said it was raining an awful lot. He said he was thinking of going to the dance in the College, but the rain gave him the thought that he would stay in. So I said we would play the table-tennis together until the bedtime."

Montero recovered himself from the plethora of definite articles with which Indians tend to adorn their English conversation.

"Where is the table-tennis room?" he asked.

"Downstairs, please. We went back down those stairs he had come up, and played for half an hour. Then Robert said he must go because he had a girl visiting here and he had to be sure she was gone out by the proper time. So we said good night."

"Did you go upstairs with him?"

"Oh no, my room is on the other side. I went out in the rain and got very wet before I had regained my own quarters."

"What you've told us may have helped a lot. Just one question—was the porter in his desk when you met Robert?"

"Yes, he was there."

"Did he see you two together."

"Oh no, I went over to Robert as he came to the top of the back stairs. They are away behind the desk. He could not have seen."

They parted with profuse thanks and expressions of goodwill on both sides. Montero and Springer had another look at the entrance hall. What the Indian had said was right: anyone could come down from the upper floors and follow the stairs down to the basement without being seen from the porter's desk. The basement, as in many houses of its period, was below the level of the street in front but opened directly on the courtyard at the back.

"So he was in the house at ten-thirty, sir," said Springer, "and went back to his room by a way that hid him from the porter in the hall. What are the odds on him now?"

"A little shorter than they were, I'll admit. It could

look as if he'd given himself a nice alibi up to the time of the murder, then made the excuse to get away so that he could go up and kill her. But if I'd planned a murder as coolly as that, I don't think I'd have made a dramatic exit down the fire-escape. I would have put myself in the convenient position of being the one to find the body."

"But don't forget, sir, that Latham was at his door a few minutes later. It's not so easy to explain away being with a new corpse behind a locked door. The timing was taken out of his hands by that. Besides, he may well have lost his nerve altogether after doing it."

At this point, Ludlow came downstairs towards them, looking rather pleased with himself.

"Good morning," he said cheerfully, "how are the clues?"

"Accumulating, Mr. Ludlow," said Montero, "and I'd like to ask you a question, if you please. Are you the owner of car number AYZ 869?"

He suddenly realised that this was the type of question he had not asked since he was a constable on the beat years ago, chasing motorists who had left their cars too long unattended.

"Yes, that's Cleopatra," Ludlow agreed, "at least, I think so, but I can never remember numbers. They form no meaningful sequence that I can see, unlike words which have a communicative and therefore a mnemonic value— but what's she been up to?"

"It's what you've been up to, Mr. Ludlow. Did you, earlier this morning, visit the lodgings formerly occupied by Jenny Hexham, and have a talk with the landlady?"

"I did. Anything wrong with that, Inspector?"

"There might be, and there might not. What is your particular interest in this case?"

"'The fact that one of my best students has come under suspicion and has been driven into hiding. I intend to find him, and clear him. And I was not aware that there is any law against talking to landladies in Shepherd's Bush on a Sunday morning."

"There's a law against interfering with witnesses. You were seen to give her money."

"I haven't your power of getting people to talk without it."

"May I ask what you found out?"

"What you had certainly already found out for yourself. That a large man, obviously disguised, though she didn't seem to realise it, had called there at nine o'clock claiming to represent Jenny Hexham and to have come for some of her things."

"All right. Now as to Robert Trent, you can safely leave it to us to find him, and to clear him *if* he's innocent. There may be bigger issues in this case than you know of. We want to get at the truth, and we shall. If you take my advice, you'll just tell us anything you happen to know and then leave the rest to us. We get paid for this."

"Yes, out of my income-tax. You go your way, Inspector, and I'll go mine. Perhaps we'll meet in the same place."

"Well if you run into trouble, don't expect us to drop everything to come and get you out. And if you show yourself *too* interested, you might find, like Polonius, that to be too busy is some danger."

Ludlow laughed. "I can join battle, Inspector, with a man who can answer me like that. You're wasting your time—Robert Trent didn't kill her."

"Perhaps you know who did?"

"Not for certain, but I'm on the way. Have another look

through your notes. And remember, what goes down must come up again."

He was out through the front door before Montero could reply. Springer sucked his teeth appreciatively. "Cor, sir," he said, "you answered him all right. You ought to have been a professor yourself."

"I'd prefer to go on enjoying English literature," said Montero.

CHAPTER V

Ludlow did not take Cleopatra with him when he set out on the first part of his search. It was well into Monday afternoon before he could slip away from the College and take the Underground to King's Cross. As he emerged into that smoky wilderness of brick and iron, he could understand the hopeless feeling of those who arrived there from far away. The confirmed Londoner learns to come to terms with his city, to accept its bustle and impersonality for the sake of all else that makes it one of the most exciting places in the world. He carves out his own little burrow, the refuge to which he can quickly return from any direction. Those who have their burrows in smaller places find it hard to see beyond the noisy rush and the apparently callous indifference of people who have to live in close proximity without intruding on each other's business or getting on each other's nerves. The great railway stations are not a happy introduction to the streets that seem to stretch endlessly in every direction. Built as proud temples of progress on the edge of the residential town, they have sucked all around them into a vortex of impermanence, a sense of perpetual transit.

Inadequately armed with Michael Hexham's instructions, Ludlow made his way along the Pentonville Road, past the barrows of doubtful fruit and the perpetually spitting groups of idlers on the street corners. Looking to right and left for anything that could possibly be called a café, he wondered how he would feel if he had just arrived perhaps from a Scottish village, with little money and no knowledge of London. Ludlow was seldom troubled with a social conscience; but his own anxiety about Robert, and the trepidation about his self-imposed task which he had concealed from Montero, gave him a surprising moment of insight. Thus meditating, he saw a dingy sign in a street to his left, proclaiming "Ted's Café". He turned towards it, shuddered at the filthy net curtains that shielded windows already opaque with dirt, and went in.

Ted, if he was the owner, was absent. His deputy was a large woman in a green overall, who leaned on a counter littered with unwashed cups and plates. Perhaps the name referred instead to the customers, a group of youths with pallid faces, long side-whiskers and the familiar pattern of pseudo-Edwardian clothing. They watched Ludlow's entry with amused hostility. Ludlow had not worked out his approach. Thinking of a café, he had imagined a neat arrangement of small tables with white cloths, plates of iced cakes and China tea—a myth reconstructed from his childhood, for he never took afternoon tea. In such conditions, he had thought, the conversation could in due time be brought discreetly round to the subject of the mysterious Hugh and his bookshop. But there was no discretion about the chipped enamel teapot in front of him or the mouldering pile of buns. He approached the counter, the guardian of which addressed him brusquely—"Yes?"

"May I have a cup of tea, please?" said Ludlow.

The youths collapsed in paroxysms of delight. Ludlow looked severely at them, as if they were erring students. The woman behind the counter half-filled a cup with milk and added a very terrible brown liquid from the teapot.

"Anything else you want?" she asked.

"No, thank you," said Ludlow.

"Naow, thenk you," chorused the youths, and again were in danger of choking with mirth at their own wit.

"Threepence, then."

Ludlow paid her, and sipped lugubriously at his cup. There was silence while the youths watched him, prepared to be derisive or aggressive as the opportunity might come. He was sure by now that his first choice had been a wrong one, yet he could not bring himself to leave without making some attempt to take his quest a little farther. Also he was rather afraid that if he did not finish his tea it might be taken as a deadly insult. He realised that his tea tasted even worse than he had expected because he had put no sugar in it. He asked for some and was rewarded with a basin of granulated sugar, crystallised around the edges into a brown crust where wet spoons had been dipped into it. The youths were further delighted by this performance. Ludlow asked the sullen woman how she liked the weather. She grimaced in some secret meaning of her own. He summoned up courage to ask his question.

"Has Hugh been in lately?"

The woman looked first blank and then suspicious.

"Who's he? Never heard of him."

Ludlow tried to look suitably conspiratorial.

"You must know him. He keeps a bookshop near here."

"I don't know nobody who keeps no bookshop," the woman replied with a truly medieval assembly of negatives that would have delighted Ludlow at any other time. He decided that it was time for him to go. Then something wet and sticky struck him on the back of the neck and a half-chewed piece of chewing-gum dropped on to his shoulder. He turned to the youths who were now quite silent, all watching him. One of them took out a knife, flicked it open and after a long look at Ludlow closed it again. He walked past their table, wondering whether his trembling was with anger or fear. As he closed the door behind him, he heard a fresh shriek of laughter from inside. He stood in the street, quite sick from emotion and perhaps from the strong tea. For a moment he felt tempted to give up his search, to go quietly back to his comfortable bachelor flat before worse happened. Then he thought that this too was London; this violence and degradation of which he had seen only the fringe was as real as the finely-bound editions that he loved. And those books had come out of experiences like this, not out of donnish talk in the Senior Common Room. He thought, too, of the boy he was looking for, alone and hunted in some place like this. He walked on and turned into another street.

With his usual ebullience he decided that a new approach must be adopted. Not for these parts were the soft manners of the college tutor. He would be tougher than they were, he thought, straightening his tall, bony figure. The next café was called "The Cremona". It was just a little less dirty than Ted's. He threw open the door with a sweep that rattled it in its frame and stood for a moment surveying the room in a way that derived from some distant memory of the Sheriff bursting into a saloon in a Western film. The occupants of the café were unmoved by his irruption. Two railway men were happy with their football coupon. A man in a seedy blue suit and a woman with a ravaged fur round her neck were quarrelling in whispers. A very thin young man was looking blankly ahead of him. This time the woman behind the counter was tall and gaunt, with a severe, rather than a sullen expression. Ludlow strode across to her and said loudly, "Tea!" The woman addressed the room in general.

"Some people," she said, "have no manners."

Ludlow modified his tactics and asked politely for a cup of tea. It proved as unpleasant as the previous one. Unwilling to abandon his new role of tough investigator, he leaned on the counter, an uncomfortable position for a man of his height, and looked around the café.

"Has anybody seen Hugh today?" he asked loudly.

Nobody showed any response. He turned to the woman behind the counter.

"Has Hugh been in here today?"

"What Hugh are you talking about?"

"Our friend who keeps the bookshop. I have a message for him from the Party."

"Whose party?"

Ludlow realised that he was on a bad wicket again. He swallowed the tea and went out reflecting what a very diverse place London is.

He could not spend the rest of the day looking for a café that might be a Communist meeting-place, if only because he was incapable of drinking any more strong tea. He decided to try to find the bookshop himself and make a direct approach to Hugh. A plaintive sound caught his ear, a street-cry of New London that deserves the attentions of a Mayhew:

"The *Daily Worker*. Read the *Daily Worker*."

Ludlow had never expected to be delighted at the sight of an angry young woman in a duffle-coat standing on a street corner. He went across to her and brushed aside the proffered copy of the paper.

"Good afternoon, Comrade," he said, before he could stop to think whether such an old-fashioned greeting was in order. "I'm looking for Comrade Hugh who keeps a bookshop near here. I have an important message for him from Headquarters. It must be given to him personally; but I have unfortunately lost the address that was given to me."

The young woman looked disapprovingly at such inefficiency but gave him the directions he wanted. He had more to ask her.

"Did you know Jenny Hexham?"

"Yes," said the girl, looking frightened, "but I never trusted her."

"You have seen the bourgeois press this morning? She was killed on Saturday."

"I know. Is that what you're going to see Hugh about?"

"My message for him is Top Secret. But do you know Robert Trent?"

"He came to one or two meetings."

"Where is he now?"

"How should I know. He's not a real Party Member. He's full of decadent liberalism."

"I see. Yes, quite so. You haven't seen him lately?"

"No. The police are after him, aren't they? I'm surprised he was the one to do it."

"Why do you say that?"

"I'm not saying any more. You'd better go and talk to Hugh if you want to. These things are too big for me."

It was clear that he would get no more from her. As he walked in the direction she had given him, he heard that forlorn call taken up again:

"The *Daily Worker*. Read the *Daily Worker*."

It was not hard to find the shop, once he knew what he was looking for. Another side street, and there was the place that Hexham had once unwillingly visited with his cousin. He had been right in saying that there was nothing in its appearance to attract attention. The frontage was as brown and peeling as might be expected, and the lettering that had once been gilt said simply and unequivocally, "Books". In the window there were a few nineteenth-century collected editions of no value; a stand full of used paperbacks stood on one side of the door, which was closed. A bell rang as Ludlow pushed it open and a man came from a recess at the back of the shop. He was in his thirties, big and dark, wearing a rough tweed jacket and brown corduroy trousers. Ludlow said that he would like to look around, and a wave of the hand encouraged him to do so. The packed shelves yielded nothing of interest either to his ordinary taste or his immediate purpose. After a while he turned back to the man, who had stayed in the shop watching him.

"You are Hugh, I suppose?" said Ludlow.

"Yes, I am."

"I don't think I know your surname."

"Does it matter?"

"Perhaps it matters a lot. I have something important to tell you and I want to tell it to the right man."

"Tell me the name of the right man, and I'll tell you if it's mine."

This was getting too difficult. He tried a new approach.

"I was told you might have some special books, not on display, that would interest me."

Hugh sighed, unlocked a cupboard at the back of the shop and brought out a few books.

"No, no," said Ludlow, "not that sort of book. Something of political interest for those who are free from bourgeois prejudices."

74

"I'm afraid I don't know what you mean, sir. We don't carry many political books. Perhaps you'd better try somewhere else."

"Look here, I'm a comrade like you."

"Indeed, sir?"

"And I've been sent to you by those who are very high in the Party."

"Most interesting, I'm sure. But if there's nothing I can do for you today . . ."

"There is. You can tell me where to find the man who killed Jenny Hexham."

There was a flash of alarm in the other man's eyes, gone as soon as it appeared.

"Hexham? I don't think I know the name."

"You know it all right. She's been here often, once with her cousin. Probably with Robert Trent too."

"The names mean nothing to me. We get such a lot of customers here."

"It doesn't look like it. And who is We—who else is concerned in this shop?"

"I'd rather like to know what right you have to ask these questions."

"I'm from Party Headquarters. And if you don't co-operate, I'll report you to the Kremlin."

Hugh's expression changed from uncomprehending distrust to a gentle and encouraging smile.

"Oh, you're from Headquarters, are you?" he said. "That's different, of course. Who exactly is the leader of your section?"

"X 22," said Ludlow desperately.

"Really? And you're investigating the death of Jenny Hexham for the Party, are you?"

"Yes."

Hugh dropped his new pleasantry. He took a step towards Ludlow.

"Now listen to me," he said. "I know who you are. You're an English don called Adam Ludlow and you've decided to stick your neck out because one of your precious students is being suspected of murder. I was warned that you were trying to follow up old trails and that you might come sniffing round here. There's nothing for you to know, and if you keep up this silly game of being a detective, you're likely to get hurt. So is your precious Robert Trent. Now get out and go back to your classroom. This stuff is too big for you."

"But surely," said Ludlow, trying to recover the ground that had suddenly dropped from under him, "you want the murderer of Jenny Hexham to be caught? I don't expect you to care about Robert Trent, because he was never in very deep with you. But the girl was one of your most devoted people, and for that alone——"

"You know a lot, don't you, Ludlow? But there are a few things you don't know and aren't going to know. We're not playing at things, if you are."

"It might be in your interest to trust me a little. I'm not concerned with your silly politics. You can talk more freely to me than you may have to talk to the Inspector in charge of this case."

Hugh's fear showed only for an instant.

"I'll gladly talk to any inspector," he said. "What can you tell him? That Jenny Hexham used to buy books at a shop kept by a man whose name you don't know—a respectable shop selling general books. Go ahead and tell him, and I might be able to fix an action for slander on you when you've finished. Go—I've got nothing to hide."

The two men looked at each other. There was a clatter at the door which made Hugh jump round convulsively. Two envelopes dropped through the letter-flap and on to the mat.

"For a man with nothing to hide, you seem to be very nervous," Ludlow said. "Or are you still hoping that the postman will bring you what wasn't found in the bracelet?"

For a moment Hugh looked as if he would strike him. He recovered himself quickly and managed to smile again.

"Yes, you do know a lot, Mr. Adam Ludlow. Perhaps you ought to be taken care of. But I'll give you a chance to get out now while you can. There are things involved in this that you don't know anything about. If you did, you wouldn't be blundering about like this—you'd be at home with your head under the clothes. And to think that I'm fighting to make a better world for people like you!"

Ludlow cautiously moved to the door and held the handle before speaking. The street outside looked reassuringly safe and sane. Even Ted's Café made more sense than this lunacy.

"I don't know whether you believe yourself," he said, "or whether you just think you can bluff people for long enough to put you into power. But either way you're wrong. I thought I might come upon something big here. Instead I've just found another of the pathetic dupes who'll be the first to go if you ever establish the system you want —they call it elimination of reactionary elements, I believe. Don't you know what kind of nihilistic destructive power you're playing with? Read some history, man, and get a bit of sense before it's too late." He opened the door for his last long shot. "I suppose you look on poor Jenny Hexham as a martyr to the great cause?"

The anger that had been rising in Hugh's face turned to astonishment.

"You fool, Ludlow," he said, "you absolute bloody fool."

Ludlow walked away quickly, feeling an uneasy tension between his shoulder-blades until he had turned the corner into the main road. The angry girl was still selling, or at least offering, the *Daily Worker*. He walked past her without recognition and hurried towards King's Cross. He felt that his afternoon had been most profitable, and well worth two cups of strong tea.

CHAPTER VI

Detective-Sergeant Springer lowered himself for the third time from the window of Michael Hexham's room. His feet touched the window-sill of room 27 immediately below. Steadying himself with one hand against the wall, he threw up the half-opened window and swung himself forward into the room. He disengaged himself from the webbing harness and let it hang loosely outside the window. A moment later, he stepped again on the sill, seized the harness and tried to draw himself up again. The strong spring relentlessly lowered him to the courtyard. Finding his feet there, he looked grimly at the escape, now extended to its full length, and started to haul himself up it like a gymnasium rope. A shout from above stopped him.

"All right, Jack," said Montero, his head appearing from Hexham's window, "come up the stairs this time."

Springer grunted and went through the back door of the building, to reappear on the top floor out of breath and rather out of temper.

"It can't be done, sir," he said. "That thing takes you right down to the ground. It's not too hard to stop at the window where there's a hold for your feet, but it's impossible to climb up again. And I doubt whether he could have handled a body down even to the next floor."

"Perhaps we ought to try it with an extra weight, to make sure."

A malicious gleam came into Springer's eyes. "I'll take

you down if you like, sir," he said. "I think I can still manage the old fireman's lift."

"We'll leave out that part of the performance," Montero said hastily. "Anyway, our combined weights would hardly be a fair substitute for those two. And I still think she was murdered in the room where she was found. But he could have got down part of the way on his own fire-escape, used Trent's as a cover to take him to the ground, come back by the stairs and rolled up his own."

"But then he'd have run into Latham and Ferris—remember that Latham is just opposite here, and went down by the stairs he'd have had to come up."

"I know. Either Ludlow's a fool or I misunderstood him. I don't know why I ever bother with these amateurs who think they know it all—unless it's because they do sometimes know a little bit that's useful."

Meanwhile Ludlow, unaware of these criticisms, had made his way back to Mudge Hall. The first person he saw there was Michael Hexham, pacing up and down the entrance hall like a sulky lion.

"Hullo," Ludlow said cheerfully, "do you know if the Inspector's anywhere about?"

"I should think I do," replied Hexham. "The two of them are up in my room trying to prove I killed her. They're going up and down the fire-escape like madmen. And it's all your fault—you said something that gave them the idea. I think it's pretty mean, after I told you all I knew. If you think you can turn suspicion on to me from Robert Trent, you're wrong."

Ludlow tried not to laugh. "I think I can soon put them right," he said, and made for the stairs.

Montero did not seem pleased to see him. "We're rather busy now, Mr Ludlow," he said.

"Yes, I can see you are. I'm awfully sorry if I started you on these exercises. It wasn't what I meant—in fact you're on the wrong level, so to speak. But I've had rather an interesting afternoon that I'd like to tell you about."

"I don't think I want to hear about how you've spent the afternoon, thank you."

"No? A pity. I suppose I must get in touch with Scotland Yard and speak to your immediate superior. What a nuisance!"

"If you have anything to tell me that might have a bearing on the murder of Jenny Hexham, I'll be glad to hear it; but not if you just want to tell me again that Robert Trent didn't do it."

"Well, I'm certain now that he didn't. But that's not all. Let's sit down, shall we."

He took the single arm-chair in the room, leaving the two detectives to perch themselves on the edge of Hexham's bed. He ran through his adventures of the afternoon, to an audience that became increasingly attentive. At the end, Montero was grudgingly impressed.

"That's certainly interesting," he said, "though you'd do much better to leave these investigations to us. If people would only co-operate with us in the first place—however. I should be very glad if you would come straight to me with anything you may learn from students. You only put yourself in danger by doing this sort of thing. And you've put this fellow Hugh on his guard—you say you don't know his surname?"

"I didn't say that," said Ludlow, who was enjoying himself very much. "You should listen more attentively. I said that he wouldn't tell me. His name is Hugh Quantrough."

The two men on the bed jerked their heads up and looked quickly at each other.

"How do you know?" asked Montero.

"Just before I left the shop, the postman pushed two letters through the door. It is an occupational disease among academics to be short-sighted, but fortunately I can see a little way beyond the end of my nose. In fact, I can see the not inconsiderable distance to my feet—and there at my feet was an envelope with his name on it."

Montero had the civility to congratulate him. "We'll have a quiet look at this fellow," he said, "though there's nothing we can pull him in for yet. Now we'd better get hold of young Hexham and find out officially about this bracelet."

"Can I stay?" asked Ludlow innocently.

Montero gave him a long look. "I suppose you may as well, since you seem to have found it out for yourself. But you mustn't interrupt."

"I'll be good," Ludlow promised. "You'll find Michael Hexham walking about in the entrance hall."

Springer was sent to fetch Michael and soon returned with him. Montero launched his attack as soon as they came into the room.

"Why didn't you tell me about your cousin's bracelet?"

"Because you didn't ask me."

"I could consider that concealing material evidence. Tell me now, all that you know."

"He can tell you," said Michael, pointing at Ludlow.

"I want to hear it from you."

Michael told the story as he had told it to Ludlow. Montero was very interested.

"Are you quite sure your cousin was wearing the brace-let when she left you on Saturday evening?" he asked.

"If she hadn't been, I wouldn't have thought later that it had been stolen, would I?"

"Please answer my question."

"Yes, she was wearing it."

"And it had gone when you came to the room where she was found?"

"Yes."

"Have you seen it since then?"

"How could I?"

"Have you seen it since then?"

"No."

"Have you been to that bookshop at King's Cross since the first time you went there with your cousin?"

"No fear. It was a rotten bookshop anyway."

"Do you know anybody called Quantrough?"

"No."

"All right, Mr. Hexham, that will do for the moment. I must ask you not to leave this address without informing us."

"All right. You're determined to get me, aren't you?"

"We are determined to solve this case and to get any information that we may need towards solving it."

"Can I come back into my room now?"

Montero nodded, and Michael Hexham flounced towards the arm-chair as Ludlow vacated it. The three men stood outside on the landing, all thinking unpleasant thoughts about the occupant of the room they had just left.

"I think I'll have another talk with that Pole," said Montero. "We'll go and see if he's in."

Steve was in fact in his room on the floor below and received them politely. Ludlow included himself in the party, and was not openly rebuked. At Montero's request,

Steve again went through his movements on Saturday evening.

"Now, think very carefully before you answer," Montero warned him, "because a lot may depend on this. Are you absolutely certain that you handed the bunch of keys to Ferris himself, and did not simply leave them on his desk?"

"I am quite, quite certain."

"Beyond all possibility of mistake?"

"I could not make a mistake about a thing like that."

"How can you be sure that it was Ferris you gave the keys to?"

"Who else should it be? He stood there, behind his desk, and when I said I had brought them back he held out his hand for them, and took them."

"Did you see his face?"

"Well, no. He was bending down behind the desk and I saw only his cap and the side of his head. He reached up over the desk for the keys."

"Did he speak to you?"

"No, he made a sort of noise, like a pig—how do you say it?"

"Grunt," said Montero and Springer together, so that Ludlow had to suppress a laugh.

"Thank you, yes, he grunted."

"Didn't it strike you as unusual that he said nothing to you?"

"Not at all. No, I am sorry that Mr. Ferris is not a very polite man. Often when we ask him for something he— yes, grunts."

"Now I want to put this to you in a slightly different way, Mr.—er—Steve. I have no reason to suppose that you wish to deceive me or to pervert the ends of justice——"

Like Brutus, Montero paused for a reply. There was no reaction, except that Ludlow looked very disapproving at hearing such a cliché from a man of whose intelligence he had come to think so well.

"Therefore," Montero went on, "since there are discrepancies in the accounts I have had of the returning of these keys, I am wondering whether you did perhaps leave the keys on the desk when Ferris was absent, and are now afraid to admit having done so. I imagine that there is a rule against leaving official keys around?"

"Yes, we must return them at once, and only give them to the porter on duty. But I assure you——"

"If that is so," Montero interrupted him, "*I* can assure *you* that we are not a bit interested in the internal discipline of this establishment. Nothing that you tell us will go any farther unless it has any bearing on this case. And if it does, I think Mr. Ludlow would be prepared to have a word with the Warden so that you didn't get into any trouble."

Ludlow, who seemed to be deeply interested in one of Steve's books that he had picked up, nodded sympathetically.

"Please, Mr. Inspector, sir, I gave the keys to the porter. That is the truth."

"Very well. I'm not satisfied, but we'll leave it there for the moment. Now tell me something else. Did you see or speak to anybody, either when you went to get the keys or when you were returning them?"

"When I went down to get them, I saw a boy called Pratt. The door of his room was open, and he asked me if I was going out please to get him some cigarettes. I said I would not go out in such rain, only I was locked from my room and had to get the keys."

"What happened then?"

"He said, 'That's your lot, Jack', and slammed his door. He is a boy who says a lot of things I do not understand."

"May I interrupt?" asked Ludlow plaintively. "I know Pratt and I talked to him and the other student in his room on the night of the murder. I don't think you need bother questioning them."

"I'll decide that later. Did he tell you about seeing this chap with the keys?"

"No."

Montero was clearly pleased with knowing something that Ludlow did not, and turned back to Steve.

"Are you sure you neither saw nor spoke to anyone else?"

"Yes, quite sure."

"Was the key that you had used still on the bunch when you returned to the porter's desk?"

"But yes."

"Did you remove it at any time when the keys were in your possession?"

"No."

"Do you know a man called Hugh Quantrough?" Montero shot the question out so sharply that it was impossible to tell whether the slight start that Steve gave was caused by alarm or surprise.

"No, I do not know that name," he said.

"Do you know any bookshops in the direction of King's Cross?"

"King's Cross? That is a station, is it not? I do not think I have ever been there."

"That's all for now." Montero looked at the others and got up. At the door he turned and said, "If you get any other ideas about those keys, don't forget to let me know."

Once again they found themselves standing vaguely on the landing.

"We'll have Ferris now," Montero said, "while all that's fresh in our minds. Bring him to the room they've given us downstairs, Jack."

"He won't be on duty now, sir."

"No, but he sleeps in the building—I found that out. Ask the man who's on now where his room is."

When Springer had gone, Ludlow followed the Inspector cautiously, like a child anxious not to be sent back from an adult outing. Montero, however, seemed preoccupied and inclined to be friendly. He made no objection when Ludlow followed him into the study-room and sat down.

"What did you think of all that?" Montero asked unexpectedly.

"He was very convincing. If I hadn't known he was lying about one thing I should have been completely taken in. Of course," he added diplomatically, "you with your greater experience can't have been deceived."

"How did you know he was lying?"

"I'll tell you that if you tell me why you looked so surprised when I mentioned Hugh Quantrough."

"It's unwise to make bargains with the police: and it's a serious thing to withhold information in a case of murder." Montero sounded severe but his eyes twinkled.

"Well, while you were busily occupied with interrogation, I took a glance at one or two of Steve's books. He seems to be reading the notably dull subject of economics, which is a mixture of common sense and witchcraft. When I ask an economist a perfectly simple question about the income-tax which is brutally extorted from my meagre salary——"

"Yes, but what about this book?" Montero was beginning to get used to Ludlow's digressions.

"It was quite an elementary textbook on the subject; even I've read it. But it so happened that, inside the front cover, there was one of those little gummed labels that booksellers use. It was from Quantrough's shop."

"With his name on it?"

"No, just the address."

Montero tried hard not to look impressed, until his native honesty overcame him.

"That was a neat piece of work," he said. "Now I'll tell you something. Perhaps I'm sticking my neck out, but you've been useful to us and I think I can trust you. Mind, this is all quite confidential, and I don't want you to get any more ideas about running this thing on your own. This morning another man called at the house where Jenny Hexham used to lodge. He asked Mrs. Reddle if he could look through her room. Now, we've got a man there to interview everybody who calls asking about her. Nobody has, since you were there yesterday. This chap seemed quite open about it. He said he was a bookseller who had sent her certain books on approval for which she had not paid. He had written to her several times without result. He affected to be completely surprised that she was dead."

"But it was all over the papers," Ludlow interrupted.

"I know, but some people don't read them. Anyway, he was quite apologetic. We asked for his name and address so that we could get in touch with him, and he gave them without hesitation. Can you guess?"

"Hugh Quantrough?"

"Right first time. We had his local station check up on him, and at the Yard too. There's nothing known. In his own district he has the reputation of being a bit of a recluse. Except for a few tradespeople who supply him, hardly anybody knew about him."

"Did you find any books bought from him, or any of the letters he said he'd sent?"

"No letters. Though we've found few letters or papers of any kind, which seems to confirm her cousin's story about her keeping everything in some secret place. There certainly were some books with his label on them. But it's pretty clear to me that he was looking for whatever it is that other people are looking for—a lot of papers that could make it awkward for a lot of people if they became public. He had a good cover story in case we had a man there, as we had. I probably wouldn't have thought any more about it except for what you've told me this afternoon."

"Could he have been the same man who was there yesterday?"

"Well, he certainly wasn't disguised today, and he tried a completely different approach. I'd say not, and I'd say too that Quantrough is a much more experienced man at this sort of thing than the one who came before."

Ludlow nodded. "I'm sure you're right," he said.

"Are you going to tell me that you know the identity of yesterday's visitor?"

"I'm not going to tell you anything, Inspector, until I'm quite certain of it. But perhaps you'll tell me something. Do you still think that Robert Trent murdered Jenny Hexham?"

"I think this case is a great deal more complicated than it seemed at first, and that a lot of people had an interest in her death. I think that there were accomplices, who are trying their hardest to get hold of her papers. But everything does point to Trent being the actual murderer. I shall feel happier when he's found and I can talk to him. So if you happen to find him in your wanderings around London . . ."

"If I find him, I'll use any influence I may have with him to get him back here to see you."

"That's good. Tell him that nothing he says can make it look any worse for him than it does at present, but that he may be able to clear himself. At the moment he's our hottest suspect, and we shall find him sooner or later. If it's sooner, that will be a great deal better for everybody —including Trent himself."

"I'll do all I can. By the way, do you think I could have a look at the girl's books?"

"Would that help you to find Trent?"

"Perhaps not. But as I'm used to dealing with books, especially in her subject, I might possibly notice if there was anything out of the way in them."

"Well, I certainly can't see anything. I've promised to let her cousin have any of her things that we don't need for further investigations."

"Is he handling her estate, so to speak? What about her parents?"

"It seems that her father's abroad. The grandmother had a severe heart attack when she heard the news and the mother has to stay with her for a day or two at least. It's a rotten business."

"Yes, it is. May I say one other thing—don't think too badly of Steve for lying about Quantrough. Remember that he comes from a country where people have learnt to have a very different idea of the police from the one we have here. He's probably terribly afraid to be suspected of any Communist association, just as up to a year ago he was afraid to be suspected of any non-Communist ones."

"I realise all that. It doesn't alter the fact that either he or Ferris is lying about something that may be the most important clue in the case."

The door was flung open. An impartial observer would have had doubts whether Ludlow's high view of the English police was justified. Springer came in, dragging a very dishevelled Tom Ferris. In his other hand, the sergeant was holding something carefully wrapped in a handkerchief. Still grasping Ferris by the arm, he revealed the object to Montero. It was a gold bracelet, wide and heavy.

"He had it in his hands when I went in, sir," Springer said. "Turning it over and gloating like a miser. He didn't have a chance to put it away."

"I didn't have a chance to do nothing," said Ferris sulkily, "with you coming into a gentleman's room like that without knocking."

"I did knock," said Springer righteously.

"Not so that anybody could hear it, you didn't."

"Never mind about that," said Montero; "will you please explain how you came to be in possession of this bracelet?"

Ferris explained at some length, with many oaths and protestations of honesty. He had been doing the boilers early on Sunday morning, his last task before handing over to the day-porter and going to bed, when he saw something gleaming in the coke. He picked it up and saw it to be a gold bracelet. He had taken it to show to the Inspector but had forgotten about it until he got up late that afternoon. He had been about to bring it up when Springer had come into his room.

"'A likely story," said Springer. "You knew where it had come from."

"How could I have known? I thought somebody had dropped it."

"Perhaps somebody did," said Montero, "or perhaps it was never in the coke at all." He turned to Ludlow. "Was he in the room when Michael Hexham said the bracelet had been stolen?"

"Yes," said Ludlow, "he was."

"Can you suggest how the bracelet could have got into the coke?"

"Must have fallen through the grating," said Ferris. "There's a sort of skylight with a grating in the court-yard."

"Let's get this right," Montero said. "The boiler-house is below street level and on the level of the courtyard at the back. Do I understand that the coke store is below that again?"

"It sort of slopes back. It runs alongside the boilers, the whole depth like. The coke comes in from the hole in the street and runs back—and a hard job it is to get it out of that bottom part."

"Is this grating directly under the back wall?"

"That's right."

"We'll take this bracelet to be identified and looked at properly. As for you, Ferris, you're not to leave this build-ing until I say so. If you so much as stick your nose out-side, I'll pull you in for stealing by finding, with the possibility of a much more serious charge coming up. Have you any objection to a search being made of your room?"

"Does it make any difference if I have?"

"Only that I have to get a warrant—and I'll keep you here under supervision while I get it."

"Go ahead and search. I ain't got nothing to hide."

"Right. Go with him, Jack."

Ferris was led out, muttering, by Springer. Montero yawned.

"We'll call it a day, I think," he said. "Don't go and get mixed up in anything in the middle of the night. I want my sleep."

"I won't," said Ludlow. "I want mine too."

CHAPTER VII

Ludlow got his sleep all right. It was as well that he did, for the following morning turned out to be an exhausting one. It began at ten by a tutorial with Pratt who, perhaps feeling that Ludlow now knew too much about him, actually arrived on time with his essay completed. After a vain attempt to steer the conversation to police methods and crime in general, he surrendered to fate and began to read.

"Chaucer was the Father of English Poetry," he began.

"Stop, stop," said Ludlow. "What does that extraordinary statement mean?"

"It means that Chaucer was the first English poet."

"Indeed? And what about the texts of the twelfth and thirteenth centuries that we have been looking at in recent weeks?"

Pratt looked pained. "But that wasn't Literature," he said, "that was Language."

They went on in this manner for an hour. Towards the end of the time, Ludlow became aware by shadows on the frosted glass panel of his door, that students were waiting outside for him to finish. He resigned himself to no coffee and another hour of miscellaneous business, for he would seldom send a student away unanswered. After dismissing the chastened Pratt, he dealt with two problems for members of the English department. The next knock on the door announced an unexpected student—Henry Prentice.

"This is an infrequent pleasure," said Ludlow. "I don't often get visits from the chemists."

"I know, sir. I think there ought to be a lot more mixing between departments, don't you? I mean, we scientists tend to get rather narrow in our outlook. And the arts man has something to learn from us too, wouldn't you agree?"

"No doubt. For my own part, I am glad enough to hold on to what I have. So far I haven't mastered my own subject as much as I should like. My time for thinking about science is not likely to come in this incarnation. I am thankful that I am still allowed a corner in which to teach, and that I have not yet been displaced by an atomic pile. No doubt it will come."

"Scientists aren't as bad as all that, Mr. Ludlow. We know that what we are doing is never an end in itself. Your kind of subject can give us the real values—that's why I wish there was more time for inter-faculty lectures and things like that."

"Your sentiments do you credit. I wish I could think that they were shared by all your fellow-scientists. Anyway, as long as we pay lip-service to something called 'general education', we shan't get very far. It isn't just a question of more lectures—it's an attitude of mind within each academic discipline. But did you come simply to talk about that?"

"No, I didn't, and I mustn't take up any more of your time. I came to ask whether you had any news of Robert Trent."

"Nothing, unfortunately, though I've a few more ideas than I had on Saturday. Have you found out anything?"

"No. I just wondered about what you had been doing since you talked to me on Saturday."

"Quite a lot, but I haven't found him. Nor have I given up searching."

"I can't help feeling that I am a bit responsible for him. I mean, if I had been able to do more for him on Saturday when he came to me, it mightn't have happened."

"What mightn't have happened?"

"Him killing her."

"His killing her," said Ludlow automatically. "So you are quite sure that he is guilty?"

"I don't want to think so—that's why I hope he'll turn up soon so that he may be able to clear himself. But it does look pretty black for him, doesn't it?"

"Yes, I'm afraid it does. But he seemed more cheerful, you said, when he left you on Saturday?"

"Yes, that's why I feel hopeful in spite of everything, because he just didn't seem in the mood to do anything silly or desperate."

"He'd quite got over his quarrel with her?"

"Well, I thought so."

"One thing perhaps you could tell me now you're here, that's just occurred to me. Those fire-escape things that go up and down in pairs—I'm afraid that's not a very scientific description, but you know what I mean—are they fitted in every room at the Hall?"

"Oh, no, only two rooms on the second and third floors. One room at the back and one at the front on each floor. Those rooms are to be used as emergency exits if necessary."

"What about you chaps on the first floor?"

"I suppose we just hang on to the window-sill and drop. There's never been a fire to test it out."

"So most of you have no ideas about how to use those escapes?"

"Yes, we have a practice about twice a year, when we all go to the top floor of the block we live in and come down on one of the escapes. It generally ends as a bit of a rag."

"Do the staff take part in these practices?"

"Yes, everybody who lives in the Hall. Well—the Warden usually stands at the bottom and watches."

"I see. I just wondered. If I find Robert Trent soon it will be a great relief to all of us."

"It certainly will. I wonder if there's anything I could do to help?"

"Thank you, but I think I'll go it alone, as the phrase is." Ludlow looked at his watch with the gesture that his own students knew well to mean the end of an interview.

"I mustn't take any more of your time," said Prentice.

"No. Good morning."

The next visitor was a girl in the English department, Sheila Broome. Ludlow prepared himself for academic matters again, but he was not to forget the other problem so easily. Sheila began at once:

"Mr. Ludlow, it isn't about work, it's about Robert. Where is he? Have you found him? Do you still believe that he's innocent?"

"Sit down, Miss Broome, and let us remember that the academic mind does not try to answer more than one question at the same time. That is excellent advice for examination candidates—I hope, by the way, that you will never be guilty of the horrid neologism 'examinees'. The answers to your questions are, respectively, I don't know, No and Yes."

This flow of words had, as it was intended to do, given Sheila time to compose herself. Now she looked a little embarrassed.

"I expect you wonder why I should be so interested. But Robert and I have been—well—friends since our first year. I haven't seen so much of him just lately. But I do hope so much that he's going to be all right."

Ludlow looked at the slight figure sitting opposite him, and felt one of his rare pangs of regret for his bachelor state. 'If I disappeared,' he thought, 'nobody would care.' Certainly no girl like this, young and fresh with all her affection still to give. He checked himself and spoke very gently.

"I understand," he said, "and perhaps you may know things that will help me to find Robert. I've no clear line yet, but at least I've done a bit of elimination."

"And you don't think he did it?"

"I'm sure he didn't. Aren't you?"

"Yes, but everybody seems to assume that he's guilty, just because he's disappeared. He may be dead, too."

"I don't think so. Just very frightened, and becoming more so."

"Do you know who did kill her?"

"What intellectual honesty remains to me compels me to say that I don't. But I have ideas, which I hope will become certainties."

"I feel so worried about him."

"I'm sure you do. But I think that everything will turn out all right. Did you know Jenny Hexham well?"

He tried to make the question sound casual. Sheila blushed and looked confused before answering.

"Not awfully well. We were in the same year, of course, and the same subject, so we saw a good bit of each other."

"Forgive the question, but it may be important: were you in any way jealous of her?"

"About Robert, you mean? Certainly she had an

influence over him, and they used to meet a lot. But I never thought somehow that there was anything—well—emotional in it. I wasn't jealous in that way, but of course I did resent the way she took up his time. And this political business he got mixed up in wasn't good for him."

"Was he worried about the way he had committed himself?"

"Yes, very. I don't think he meant to go so far as he had. I'm sure he would have got out of it, if she hadn't had such a hold over him."

"You mean she was blackmailing him?"

"I don't think so, but she had a very strong personality. She seemed to be able to get people to do what she wanted."

"When was the last time you saw her?"

"It was last Friday, the day before she—died. It's awful to think that we were talking on top of a bus as if nothing strange was ever going to happen, and next day she was killed."

"It's a nasty business," said Ludlow, inadequately. "Try to remember the conversation you had with her. You say you saw her on top of a bus?"

"I met her first at Victoria. I'd just come back from visiting an aunt at Maidstone, and I saw Jenny as I came away from the platform. When I asked if she'd been anywhere she seemed a bit put out, but I can't think why. She said she was just wandering around. We were going in the same direction for part of the way, so we got on a bus together outside the station and had quite a long talk. I thought then that she was really rather nice—quite sensible and quiet."

"Did you talk about Robert?"

"No, he wasn't mentioned. I think we'd both have liked to really, but neither of us would start."

"How did she seem then? You say she was fairly quiet —was it in a happy sort of way, or a frightened one?"

"Well, now you mention it, she did seem a little bit frightened, but quite cheerful too. As if she'd done something she had been putting off for a long time."

"Can you remember exactly what she was doing when you first saw her at the station?"

"She was just standing, in that big open part in front of the platforms. I remember that she was just closing her handbag."

"Did you notice whether she was wearing a bracelet?"

"That big gold one? Yes, she always wore it. It was stolen, wasn't it, when she was killed?"

"Yes. Thanks for all that. Now what are we going to do about Robert? Have you any suggestions?"

Sheila looked very cheered at being included in Ludlow's investigations.

"Well, as a matter of fact," she said, "I did wonder whether he'd gone back anywhere near his old lodgings. But I expect you've been there?"

"I haven't, because I know nothing about them."

"He wasn't in Mudge Hall for his first year——"

"I know, I used some influence with my colleague Blake to get him in, as he was a likely young man. I thought a bit of the community life would do him good. It is really surprising how influence and patronage spreads to the most trivial—I beg your pardon for interrupting you. Please go on."

"Robert liked his digs, though he was very pleased to get into the Hall. I think he made quite a few friends around there, and he used to go back to see them sometimes. I thought it was just possible that he might have gone there. He didn't go about an awful lot, and he'd be more likely to go somewhere that he knew. That is, assuming he hasn't gone home, but I suppose the police have found out about that."

"I've no doubt that they have. Your deductions are admirable, Miss Broome, and you may be on the right track. If I remember rightly, his lodgings were somewhere in Streatham. I suppose you haven't any record of the address?"

"Yes, I looked in an old diary of that year and found it." Looking confused and consequently very pretty, Sheila produced a piece of paper and gave it to him.

"Thank you very much. I think I'll follow this up as soon as possible."

"I hope you don't think it's too awful of me to come and see you like this." Sheila got up to go.

"I'm glad you have so much confidence in me. And you've given me two useful bits of information."

"Two—only the address, surely?"

"You've also given me a pretty good idea of what I'm looking for—and this time I don't mean Robert."

"I don't suppose—oh, please Mr. Ludlow, can't I come with you to look for him?"

"It would be better if you didn't, for many reasons. At least, not until I'm nearer finding him. But I'll tell you when there's anything to be told. Before you go, do you know Robert's friend, Henry Prentice?"

Sheila blushed for the third time that morning.

"I've just come to know him," she said. "He's—well, asked me to go out with him. I think I will, I mean it can't help Robert if I stay in all the time, can it?"

"Certainly not. I suppose you met Prentice through Robert?"

"No, I didn't know they were particular friends. He just spoke to me and asked me. Of course, I've known him for a long time in an ordinary sort of way. He's very clever, and supposed to be ambitious, too. I think he's rather nice—very gentle and kind."

"Well, that seems very satisfactory. I hope very much that I'll have some news of Robert for you before long. Good morning, Miss Broome."

Ludlow decided to get away before he had any more callers. As he got up and started putting a few papers in his brief-case to take away, there was a bulkier shadow outside the door, and a more peremptory knock on it than would announce a student. Montero came in before Ludlow could get his hat and look as if he was just going.

"Good morning to you," Montero said cheerfully.

"Oh dear," said Ludlow, "this is developing into one of those mornings. What have I done now?"

"Nothing amiss I hope and believe. This is just a visit from a stranger to academic life who finds himself a bit out of place in all these learned corridors. May I sit down?"

Although he sat in the chair in which many students had heard their essays mercilessly dissected, he managed to give the impression that it was he who was conducting the interview. Ludlow subsided into his arm-chair on the other side of the desk.

"I'd just come in for a look round," Montero explained, "when I saw your name on the list of rooms at the end of this corridor, so I thought I'd drop in. I hope I'm not keeping you from anything important?"

"Not at all," said Ludlow.

"There might be something to find out by wandering around. After all, this college is where the murdered girl—and quite possibly the murderer too—spent a good bit of their time. One might get something from notice-boards, scraps of conversation, anything. Besides, I rather like the academic atmosphere."

"So do I. Have you found anything useful?"

"Perhaps. This is a pleasant room. So this is where you put them through it?"

"It's more often they who put me through it," Ludlow said. He knew that all this small-talk was leading up to something, and it soon came.

"That was a pretty little thing who was coming away from here just before I came in," Montero said casually. "Do you get many like that?"

"Who—oh, Sheila Broome. Yes, she's a nice child and moderately intelligent. She's rather keen on Robert Trent."

"Is she, now? Well, of course, that explains it."

"Explains what?"

"Why she was hanging about his old lodgings yesterday. She went in for a time, but her face when she came out was enough to tell our man who was watching that he wasn't there."

"Did she know she was being watched?"

"My dear fellow, give us credit for a little skill in our methods."

"So you've investigated his former lodgings?"

"We have. Your tone tells me that you haven't and were intending to. Go ahead by all means, but I don't think you'll learn anything. For your information, we have also been to his home and to most of his known haunts. A thorough search of his room gave us quite a lot of lines to follow, but they haven't led anywhere—yet."

"Then there's no harm in my trying a bit more, is there?"

"Probably not, as long as you realise that this is a dangerous business. It's not just a recreation for tired academics, like doing crossword puzzles. Whoever is behind this murder hasn't finished his job until he gets what he's looking for."

"What was in the bracelet, you mean?"

"Presumably. By the way, we've had it identified by her cousin and one or two people who knew her, and it's hers all right."

"Do you think Ferris took it in the first place, or that he found it as he said?"

"When we're sure about that, we'll be a lot farther on than we are now. If he took it, he killed her and probably did it for the value of the gold. If he found it, somebody else killed her for the value of whatever was inside that bracelet, and threw it down when he'd either found or failed to find it. The interest that certain people have been taking in her lodgings suggests that he didn't find it and is still looking for it."

"What about fingerprints?" asked Ludlow, hoping to sound knowledgeable.

"It was covered with ones from Ferris, of course. Anything else had been wiped out by his—he must have fingered it and gloated over it pretty thoroughly. There's nothing to go on there."

"No marks inside that might be a code or anything?"

"We've had it under the microscope. We've given every test our laboratory knows. There's nothing. Something must have been hidden inside it. I wish I knew what."

"Did the murderer know, or was he just hoping?"

"Ask me another, Mr. Ludlow. I don't know where we

go from here, and that's a fact. I won't deny that I was hoping you might have something for me, since you seem to have a way of turning up information about this case."

Ludlow pressed the tips of his fingers together and looked thoughtfully at the ceiling.

"To be concealed under a bracelet that was being worn," he said, "it would have to be something small something thin and capable of being folded."

"Yes, of course. A scrap of paper of some kind, probably."

"Quite. Something, perhaps, about the size of a railway cloakroom ticket."

Montero sat upright with a start. "That's a very shrewd idea," he said. "May I ask how you came by it?"

"Just by listening," said Ludlow modestly.

"You don't happen to know what's at the other end of the ticket?"

"I don't know that it's a ticket at all, but I think it may be. Now you tell me something, if you will. If I go and have another talk with Mrs. Reddle at Jenny's lodgings, will you arrest me?"

"No," said Montero, smiling, "but I won't give you any money from the funds to bribe her either. If you can get anything worthwhile out of her, it's more than we've been able to do."

"I'd like to try, anyway," Ludlow said.

"So you shall. I'll give our man there the word that you'll be coming. But I want him to be present at any conversation you may have with her."

"Fair enough." Ludlow looked pointedly at his watch.

"I can take a hint," Montero said. "I'll see you again before this case is finished. Be good."

When he had gone, Ludlow did not show his previous

haste to get out of the building before there were any more callers. He sat back and looked at the well-filled bookcase as if something was growing in his mind. It failed to emerge, and with an impatient shrug he got up, reached for his hat and left. He had scarcely reached the end of the corridor, when somebody stepped in front of him. It was Steve, very agitated.

"Mr. Ludlow, please excuse me that I stop you," he said.

"I haven't much time now——" said Ludlow.

"Please excuse me, this is important. There is danger in these things—danger everywhere. I see that Inspector coming from your room. Please, what did you tell him about me?"

"We didn't speak of you at all."

"If not now, then the day before. Why did you look at my books? Why did you tell him that I had been to that shop? Is there any harm that I should go and buy a book there?"

"Is there any reason why you should deny having gone?"

"In this thing there are reasons of which you can know nothing. But I see it well, that you are against me too."

"Understand this," said Ludlow firmly. "I'm not against anybody. I am very much for Robert Trent, who's getting a rotten deal out of this. For his sake, I am against the murderer, whoever he may be."

"Ah, you do not understand. In these things, it is not one or two who will suffer but all. I ask you, I implore you, to seek no more. There is big danger here."

"Danger to me, or to you?"

"To both, perhaps. The men who interest themselves in this are dangerous men."

"Men like your friend Hugh Quantrough, perhaps?"

Steve went white and leaned against the wall. "I do not know of who you speak," he said. "I have warned you. That is all."

He was gone the next moment. Ludlow walked on more slowly. He was not by any means an exceptional coward, but he had no enthusiasm for danger that could be avoided. He felt tempted to give up and leave everything to Montero. He remembered making various remarks, at academic conferences and committees and in the Senior Common Room, about the tutorial duty that did not begin and end with the hour of the lecture. There was going to be a lot more work for him, perhaps danger too, if he was ever going to be able to say those things again. He could not go back now, with one of his pupils murdered and another driven into hiding by suspicion. To find Robert and get his story of those last few minutes on Saturday evening—everything now depended on that. He straightened his lean shoulders and went out into the forecourt of the college to wrestle with Cleopatra's obstinate starting-mechanism.

CHAPTER VIII

There are parts of Streatham that keep a certain Edwardian charm and quietness within a few yards of one of the main thoroughfares out of London to the south. Making a perilous right-hand turn out of the High Road, Ludlow drove down a street that sloped away gently as if taking its time about falling into decay. The terrace of gabled houses dozed in the watery October sun, dreaming of a time before there were cars parked along the kerb and television aerials along the skyline. The stillness after the roar and strife of traffic affected him so that he drew Cleopatra to as silent a stop as her ancient brakes permitted. He sat at the wheel for a moment, looking at the house he had come to visit. Its curtains were of green plush, drawn close, with a suggestion of rooms beyond that contained aspidistras and arm-chairs with tasselled fringes. On the opposite pavement, a man in a shabby raincoat shuffled past, apparently scouring the gutter for cigarette ends. The police watch was still being discreetly kept. Ludlow got out, opened the iron gate, stepped over the few cracked tiles that made a path and rang the bell. It pealed far off, as if in lonely announcement of a messenger who had come too late to a deserted house. One of the ground-floor curtains twitched slightly. This was no world of Mrs. Reddle, where an unexpected ring brought screams and scampering feet. Mr. and Mrs. Tanner—for that was the name Sheila had given him—lived without fear of uncollected rents and persistent debts. But fear had struck here too, a mounting fear that began with news of a murder that should never have touched them. For them, as for others, the fear was not yet ended. The door opened a crack, to reveal a tired woman who looked up at Ludlow from below the level of his shoulder.

"Mrs. Tanner?"

"Yes, what is it now?"

"I'm making a few inquiries about Mr. Robert Trent, who used to lodge with you——"

"Mr. Trent ceased to be a paying guest here over a year ago. I don't know where he is now. I don't know anything about him. I told the police and I told that girl who came here, and now I'm telling you. I don't know." This is the difficulty of coming after the official investigators have done their worst, Ludlow thought. This was not a situation to be redeemed by the offer of a pound, for these people did not take lodgers. They had only paying guests. He tried a new tactic.

"That's a pity," he said. "I am anxious to help Mr. Trent and I thought you might know something about him. I understand that he has been back here to visit you since we left. However, perhaps you do not feel well-disposed enough towards him to help him in his present difficulty. I am sorry to have disturbed you."

Mrs. Tanner reacted as he had hoped. "What do you mean by suggesting that we're not well-disposed to him?" she asked. "He's a really nice young gentleman—we thought of him quite as one of the family. I don't believe all the talk that he killed that girl. And if he did, I dare say she led him on and deserved it. I'm not going to say anything to get him into more trouble."

"I'm very glad, because my wish is to get him out of

the trouble he is in already. I, too, am sure that he's innocent. I believe that his only danger is in hiding as if he were guilty. If I can find him, I'm sure he will be able to clear himself. I wonder if I could come in and talk to you for a few minutes."

A quick glance across the road told him that the man in the shabby raincoat had stopped and was apparently examining the frontages with great interest. Mrs. Tanner hesitated, then made up her mind and opened the door wider.

"You'd better come in and see Mr. Tanner," she said. "He's been poorly for the last few days and stayed off from work. Harold! Here's a gentleman asking about Mr. Trent. Says he wants to help him."

Harold rose unsteadily as Ludlow entered the room which, in spite of the promise of the neat curtains, was untidy to the point of discomfort. The grate was uncleared and the remains of breakfast, or possibly supper, lay greasily on one corner of the table. Harold was short and fat, bulging coatless over his blue trousers. He did not look at all unwell; indeed his face was red and only a slight glaze in the eyes and unsteadiness in the speech suggested any departure from perfect health. Mrs. Tanner deftly scooped up a bottle under her overall as she came in. When his first suspicions had been calmed, Harold Tanner was communicative. He agreed with his wife that Robert was a nice young gentleman and that they had thought highly of him.

"We were really sorry to see him go," he said. "He's been back though to see us. Very good of him, I said to Mrs. Tanner, to remember us when he's with all them scholars."

Ludlow could not accept this as a fair description of the majority of his pupils, but he let it pass.

"When did he last come to see you?" he asked.

"Let me see, now, it must have been last July. No, earlier, June more like. Yes, June it was. I remember him saying he was going on a holiday in July, next month as it was then. One of them Russian countries I think it was."

"And you haven't seen him since then—he hasn't been anywhere near here as far as you know?"

Ludlow had forgotten his own admonition to Sheila about asking only one question at a time. Mr. Tanner winked heavily.

"I'll take my oath in any court of law in this country," he said, "that I ain't seen young Mr. Trent since last June. As to the rest, well if you ask me no questions you'll be told no lies."

"Look here," said Ludlow, "it's of the greatest importance that I should find him before the police do. It can be only a short time now before they catch up with him, wherever he is. He can't stay in hiding for ever. If he goes to them voluntarily there's some chance of his statement being believed. And those who are behind this murder may think it in their own interest to stop him from ever reappearing and making that statement. If you want to tell the police, I've no right to interfere. Otherwise, I beg you to tell me."

Mr. Tanner looked with great concentration at his wife, as if he had never seen her before. She nodded slightly. He nodded back and addressed his next remark to her.

"I reckon he ought to go and see Short Arse."

Mrs. Tanner showed no surprise at this cognomen but merely nodded again.

"Right," said Tanner, turning again to Ludlow, "now you go and do that. You go and see Short Arse. If Mr. Trent's been anywhere around here, and I don't say he has, mind, and I don't say he hasn't, that's the man who'll know. His nephew was a pal of Mr. Trent when he lived here. Now you go back up to the main road and turn left, that's up the hill towards London, and about two hundred yards up you'll come to the Green Man. That's a public house," he kindly explained.

"Yes," said Ludlow, "I've got that. Will this—er—friend of yours be there?"

"He'll be there all right, never misses. I'd come with you myself, only I'm off work see, and you know how people gossip if they see you out. I like a drink myself, not that I drink, if you see what I mean."

Ludlow nodded his understanding of this distinction.

"Right, you go to the Green Man, straight into the saloon bar, and he'll be there. Just ask the lady behind the bar for Short Arse, and she'll point him out to you. Say Harold Tanner sent you, and then you'll see what you shall see."

Ludlow thanked him and returned to Cleopatra. As he drove away, there were encouraging waves from the Tanners and a morose scrutiny from the man in the raincoat, who was presumably preparing a description of him for Montero. As he turned back into the main road, Ludlow reflected what a complex series of small communities made up the great mass of London. Here were people sufficient to themselves in their own local streets, knowing each other's business and fearing each other's gossip. They had probably never penetrated into the dismal area around King's Cross. The pub that might seem so impersonal to a stranger was their familiar club. And here it was, the Green Man, with its name in small letters and the name of the brewers who owned it in big ones. Ludlow stopped outside, mentally adding two pounds to his expenses for parking in the wrong place, and went through the door into the saloon. It was surprisingly full, and he realised that it was nearly one o'clock. He looked round the smoky room where people sat or stood with their drinks. There seemed to be no exceptionally short man among them, so he resigned himself to asking the barmaid. 'I suppose she won't mind,' he thought, 'it's presumably the way they talk around here and think nothing of it.' He made his way to the bar where, after an interval long enough to remind him that he was a stranger, a tall, middle-aged woman came to serve him.

"Yes, please?" she asked, with a tone that suggested she disapproved strongly of all this drinking.

"I'm looking for Short Arse," Ludlow said, enunciating the words carefully. The woman's eyebrows went up.

"Who?"

"Short Arse. I understand that he's a regular customer here. He is a friend of Mr. Harold Tanner."

"Ah," said the barmaid with deep understanding. "Mr. Shorthouse is sitting at that table by the window. Do you want a drink yourself."

Cursing the corruptions of cockney pronunciation, Ludlow got himself some beer. He crossed the room to the man that had been pointed out to him, an elderly man with a grey moustache.

"Excuse me, are you Mr. Shorthouse?"

"Yes. Who are you?" Mr. Shorthouse was evidently a man of few words until he was sure of his ground.

"Mr. Harold Tanner suggested that I should come and have a talk with you. He thought you might be able to help me."

Mr. Shorthouse became expansive at once.

"If you're a friend of Harold's," he said, "you're a friend of mine. One of the best is Harold. Sit down, have a drink. Oh, you've got one. Yes, he's one of the best, is Harold."

"He said he was sorry he couldn't join us, but he was supposed to be off work."

"Ah, you've got to be careful. There are some nasty-minded people around here, the sort who think if you can come out for a drink you can be at work—which ain't true by a long way, as you well know yourself. It's all right for me, being retired, but Harold's got to be careful. Now, you say that you're in trouble and maybe I can help you?"

Ludlow explained that he was in no particular trouble but that he hoped for news of Robert Trent. Shorthouse admitted his acquaintance with Robert but was unwilling to go any farther.

"How do I know," he asked, "that you're not from the police?"

"Do I look like a policeman?"

"That's more than you or I can say. There was a time once when you only had to look at their feet and you knew. Now they're that artful, it's easy to be taken in."

"Here's my card. If you know where Robert is, or know anybody who does know it, show him this and he'll tell you who I am. Whether he'll be willing to come and meet me I don't know, because it depends how badly frightened he is. But he'll certainly tell you that I'm not a policeman and that you can trust me. Then you can decide whether you want to tell me more."

The production of a visiting-card apparently convinced Shorthouse that Ludlow was a private detective. He put it carefully into his wallet and promised to see what he could do.

"But there's no knowing," he said pessimistically. "Life is uncertain, and all things come to an end." He sighed at his empty glass, which Ludlow refilled for him. This produced another flow of optimism.

"If there's anybody who knows anything," he said, "it'll be my young nephew Bert. Very friendly he was with your young lad when he lived here. A nice boy that Robert, no side about him. He and Bert often used to come up here for a pint and a game of darts. He lives two doors from the Tanners, does Bert. 'Course, he'll be at work now, but I tell you what I'll do. I'll drop in and see him when he comes back and if he knows anything —I'm saying *if*—I'll have him up here this evening. We'll see what he's got to say—*if* he's got anything and *if* he feels like saying it. Eight o'clock suit you?"

Overwhelmed by all these If clauses, Ludlow said that it would suit him very well. Entering deeply into the spirit of the thing, Shorthouse suggested they should arrange a signal "in case the cops are trailing us", but Ludlow assured him that no cops could prevent them from meeting for a talk in a pub. They parted in great friendship, agreeing to meet again at eight.

Rather to his surprise, Ludlow found that nobody had arrested Cleopatra for obstruction and he was able to drive her away unchallenged. His course now lay north-west, to Shepherd's Bush. The beer swirled in his stomach with a sourness that reminded him that he had had no lunch, but there were things to be discovered before the evening and he drove on resolutely. The policeman on duty at Mrs. Reddle's house had had his instructions from Montero and made no difficulty about admitting him, but insisted on sitting down with them, his notebook opened. Ludlow had been afraid that Mrs. Reddle's uncertain temper would have been frayed by constant questioning, but she greeted him as an old friend and became confidential at once in spite of the presence of the constable.

"It's nice to see you again, dear," she said. "Can't call the house my own nowadays, with these fat policemen in and out all the time. But it's nice to see an old friend."

She glared at the constable, who was in fact rather thin. Ludlow did not feel that their encounter on the doorstep entitled him to be regarded as an old friend. He put a brave face on it and tried to adopt his Private Detective manner.

"Mrs. Reddle, I believe I can solve the murder of Jenny Hexham if I can learn more about what she was like when she was alive. Now you, I am sure, would take a motherly interest in any young people who were living with you and perhaps you can help me."

Mrs. Reddle preened herself. "I always try to do my best," she said. "And there's no denying that Jenny and I were good friends. Many a time she'd come into the kitchen for a nice cup of tea when she came back late. Yes, she was a nice girl, and it's a shame she's gone." She wiped her eyes dramatically.

"Forgive me, but when I spoke to you on Sunday, I got the impression that you did not think a great deal of Jenny and rather disapproved of some of her activities."

"Well, you know how it is yourself, dear, when something happens all of a sudden. You don't want to get mixed up in anything, and you think you'll put yourself as far away from it as possible. But seeing as I *am* mixed up in it, with half the police force tramping their great boots over my clean floors, I'm not going to say a word against the poor girl."

Ludlow mentally rejected the claim to clean floors but outwardly looked sympathetic and waited for Mrs. Reddle to go on, which she did.

"Of course, I'm not saying she was a saint, but then we aren't, are we? She liked a bit of fun, and what healthy girl doesn't? We have some good cries together over our boy-friends, she and I—and some good laughs too when it had all come right."

The vision of Mrs. Reddle and her boy-friends was almost too much for Ludlow and even for the well-trained constable. Recovering himself, and with a sad thought for Mr. Reddle languishing in Wormwood Scrubs, he returned to the attack.

"I suppose you know that Jenny Hexham was a member of the Communist Party?"

"Well, what of it? That ain't a crime, is it?"

"No. It may have some bearing on her death though, because some people would be happier if it was. Did she talk much to you about it?"

"Oh, I've never been much of a one for politics. Reddle—when he's here—he gets quite worked up about it, but I don't care. What's it matter, I always say. *They* will always come out on top."

"Did any of her friends from that party ever call here?" Ludlow asked, without attempting to sort out this interesting bit of political theory.

"Not that I know of. I never took no notice. I had an idea it wasn't all quite respectable, but as long as it didn't interfere with me, I didn't see any call to interfere with it. She was getting fed up with it herself though."

"Was she indeed?" Ludlow leaned forward.

"Yes, she said she was going to give it up. And she said there'd be surprises for a few people when she did."

"What do you think she meant by that?"

"I don't know. I think she had some papers that could get people into trouble if they got to the police. But I never paid much heed."

"Do you think she could have been using them to blackmail anybody?"

"Not Jenny. She wouldn't do a low trick like that. She was an open, free-handed sort of girl, even if she wasn't all some people might think she ought to be."

"You mean with her—boy-friends?"

"Well, it's only natural, isn't it?"

"I'm sure it is. Now, did any of them ever come here—or did you meet any of them elsewhere?"

"Not that I remember. She used to keep things separate —one thing in one place was good enough for her, and so it is for me. Live and let live, that's what I always say."

"Yes, yes, but can't you remember anything about these men—their names or anything?"

"They come and go and one name's much the same as another. They were students mostly, though I think one of them was one of her teachers. We used to laugh over that. And there was one she was really scared of, just towards the end. Now he was a student, and he was one of them Commies too. She had the wind up about him all right—said she wouldn't be surprised if he tried to poison her."

The young constable caught his breath and scribbled furiously. Ludlow looked interested but unexcited.

"You can't remember this one's name?" he asked.

"Not for the life of me—it was a common enough name."

"You mean like Smith or Jones?"

"Oh, not that sort of name. We never bothered using them. I mean like John or Bill—only it wasn't, I don't think."

Ludlow decided that there was nothing more to be got out of her, and as he could not take much more of her conversation he thanked her and got up to go. Mrs. Reddle insisted on seeing him to the door, gloomily watched by the constable who could see more hard work arising out of what he had just heard. It was far too late for lunch and Ludlow decided to return to his flat and sleep for a couple of hours. Combining a number of interests with his academic life, he had learnt how to shut things off his mind when necessary and concentrate on something new. It was not long before he was asleep. He awoke much refreshed and ready for an evening at the Green Man. He dined alone, at a little restaurant that had the advantages of opening early and being run by a proprietor who knew when to talk and when to keep silent. He refused his usual half-bottle of wine. The evening might contain a good deal of beer.

He arrived at the Green Man just before eight, and entered the saloon bar to find a small committee waiting for him. Mr. Tanner was not there, no doubt fearing acid comments about his absence from work, but Mr. Short-house was presiding with an air of great importance over his usual table. He had been joined by a spotty youth with a thin neck, whose hand was tightly held by a girl wearing an alarming mauve dress. When Ludlow approached them, Shorthouse looked round with an air of exaggerated conspiracy. Satisfied that there were no spies in the bar, he beckoned and pointed to an empty chair by him. He was happily unaware of the man in the raincoat who had been watching the Tanners' house that morning and was now seated a few yards away from them. He was too far to overhear a normal conversation so Ludlow ignored him and joined the group at the table. Introductions proved that the spotty youth was "my nephew Bert" and that the girl was "his friend Lorna", after which she took no further part in the conversation except to giggle admiringly whenever Bert spoke. Shorthouse opened the proceedings.

"It's all right," he said. "I showed your card to young Bert here, as soon as he got back from work, and he said it was all right to tell you. He's heard of you, from Robert."

"Often used to talk about you," said Bert, "when he was living down here. Said you were one of the best—very good to him you were, he said. Always coming out with some of the funny things you used to say. I reckoned you must be a proper card. Funny thing, though, I never knew you were a private detective. I always thought from what he said that you were one of his teachers at College."

Ludlow decided to let it pass. "Do you know Robert Trent very well?" he asked.

"We're good pals. When he lived down here, we often used to come up here for a drink. Sometimes, Saturday afternoons, we'd go to see the Palace playing at home. That was before he got mixed up with this Commie business—that didn't give him time for nothing."

"That's politics for you," interposed Shorthouse, "interferes with a man's regular habits. Don't touch it, Bert my lad, don't touch it."

"Did he talk to you much about Communism when he came to see you after he left?"

"He used to start on it," said Bert, "but he could soon see it didn't cut any ice with me. Mind, I know my rights and I see I get them, but there's no need for all that stuff. I think he was getting pretty fed up with it himself too. Last summer he talked about giving it up."

"Have you seen him more recently than the summer?"

"Now that's the question, isn't it?" said Bert with a knowing look. Shorthouse looked approvingly at his caution and Lorna giggled.

"It is the question," Ludlow said, "and I hope very much that you can tell me the answer to it. Because Robert's only hope is of getting to the police before they get to him, and I may be able to persuade him of that if I can talk to him."

"Well, seeing that Robert always spoke well of you, I'll tell you. I saw him last Sunday morning. My, he was in a state. Soaking wet and looked as if he'd seen a ghost. He turned up at our house just before dinner. Said he'd got into some kind of trouble at College and had run away. We dried his clothes and gave him dinner. We didn't know then it was anything to do with the police. He slept with us, Sunday night—on a sofa in the front room. Monday morning, he was gone—slipped out before me old dad got up, and he's an early one. Left a note on the sofa, said he couldn't stay with us and we'd know why when we saw the morning paper. And we did."

Bert paused for breath and looked important. Ludlow tried to hide his disappointment.

"Have you told anybody else, perhaps the police?" he asked.

"What call have we got to tell anybody? We keep

ourselves to ourselves. I wouldn't split on a pal in a spot of trouble. He never killed her, not Robert—he's not that sort."

"That's what I think too. I'm very grateful to you. Have you any idea at all where he may have gone when he left you?"

Bert and his uncle looked at each other. Shorthouse nodded heavily and winked at Ludlow. Bert took a breath and began again.

"I'm not claiming to know anything I don't. He may have gone to Russia for all I know. But I'll tell you this. Sunday night we sat up talking, and I asked him what he was going to do. He said he'd no money, he'd come away and left everything. Could I think of a job for him? Well, that wasn't easy, him not being trained to anything and not having his cards. But it so happened Saturday night I'd been up the Rosebud—me and Lorna often go up there—and I'd noticed they had an advert up outside the door for waiters. Lorna kidded me, I ought to have a go, to get some extra money, like. I said, I got enough work to keep me busy, thank you very much——"

"But what is this Rosebud?" Ludlow broke in, unable to bear it any longer. "Is it a public house, or a res-taurant?"

"What, the old Rosebud? Mean to say you don't know the Rosebud? He don't know the Rosebud," he announced to the others.

"Tell him, Bert," said Shorthouse kindly. "Even the detectives can't know everything. London's a big place, you know."

"Everybody knows the Rosebud. It's a palais."

"A what? Oh, I see—a dance-hall."

"That's right. Smashing one. You know Lew Tatters?"

"I don't think I do."

"You ain't half square. His band plays at the Rosebud."

"And you think Robert may have gone to work for this Mr. Tatters?"

"He don't own the place. They wanted waiters for the drinks—soft drinks like, nothing any good. They wouldn't be particular who they took on. They're always changing there, and I reckon they're glad to get what they can. You don't get many tips in a place like that—people like us who go there can't afford to live posh."

Ludlow thought this was a good moment to refill the glasses, which he did in spite of maidenly protests from Lorna. Settled again at the table, he asked for further details of the Rosebud. It was apparently to be found in a street that curved round from Tottenham Court Road to Oxford Street. There was dancing nightly, but Friday and Saturday were the big nights.

"Had Robert ever been to this place?" Ludlow asked.

"We went there a couple of times when he was living down here. He didn't care much about dancing, but his girl-friend liked it. They used to come along with us sometimes."

"Was that girl-friend called Jenny Hexham?"

"The one that's been killed? No, not her, I never saw her. This one was called Sheila. I don't know her other name."

"I know who you mean. Has he been there lately?"

"Well, not with me. I said, the politics seemed to keep him pretty busy. This girl that was killed used to keep him up to the mark on that."

"Did he say anything about her when you saw him on Sunday?"

"No. We didn't know about it then."

"Are you sure nothing was said about her? Try to remember—it may be very important."

There was a long pause while Bert looked first sullen and then uncomfortable. Ludlow knew that he was wondering whether to say any more and said nothing for fear of distracting him. At last he spoke.

"I asked him about her. He just said she was dead—didn't say she'd been murdered or anything, nor even when it was. But I thought there was something up by the way he said it. He said, 'There was a time when I'd have been glad, but it's too bad that it should happen now.' Those were his very words."

"Thank you, Bert, that tells me something I wanted to know."

"I didn't ought to have told you that."

"Why not? I can guess what's in your mind. If he knew on Sunday morning that she was dead, it looks as if he'd been the one who did it. There was nothing in the papers."

"It might have been on the radio," said Shorthouse.

"I happen to know that it wasn't. Also that he wasn't in his hostel when it was discovered. But don't worry about that. He had good reason to know that she'd been killed, but he didn't kill her. I'm really very grateful to you; you've made it possible for me to save Robert if I act quickly. What time does this Rosebud shut?"

"Eleven: half past on Saturdays."

"You've got time for another one," said Shorthouse basking in the praise given to his favourite nephew.

While Shorthouse was getting the drinks and Lorna had politely excused herself, Bert leaned over confidentially to Ludlow.

"Will you tell me something?" he asked.

"Certainly, if I can. You've told me a great deal."

"Well, it's this—how do you get all them women?"

"Women?" said Ludlow, helplessly.

"I know about you secret agents and private detectives. I've read about all of you—James Bond, Mickey Spillane, Phillip Marlowe—the lot. You're always meeting smashing blondes and getting off with them. How do you do it? What have you got that I haven't? Must be some sort of a gimmick."

"Yes," said Ludlow, "I suppose it's a sort of gimmick."

The reappearance of their companions saved him from any further need to teach Bert the difference between fact and fiction. Eventually he managed to disentangle himself and, refusing other offers of a drink, left the bar amid shouts of good-will. Shorthouse had by now abandoned his secret precautions and continued to shout instructions until Ludlow was out of the door.

As Cleopatra rattled back towards the centre of London, Ludlow felt well satisfied with himself and with the day's work. Driving slowly as he felt the fumes of the unaccustomed beer rising, he saw no reason why the case should not be finished within a few hours. The last anxiety about Robert's guilt had been dispelled. He was almost sure of the murderer, but that wanted a little more consideration. The main business was to get Robert safe and cleared; but it would be pleasant to present Montero with a complete solution to the outstanding problems. It was nearly half past nine. His flat was near Sloane Square and he decided to go there first and use the telephone. Blake had better be prepared for the return of his lost student. Also there might perhaps be a message from Montero that would make him alter his plans.

As he crossed the pavement he glanced up at his own window, for no reason that he could account for then or afterwards. Perhaps the unaccustomed glow from that particular window caught his attention. There was no doubt about it; somebody was in his flat, with a dimmed light, probably one of the reading-lamps. He went quietly up the two flights of stairs. There was nobody about: it was that dead time when the virtuous are having their suppers before going to bed and the others have not begun to think of returning. Outside his door he stopped and listened. The intruder had heard his careful footsteps, for a switch clicked inside and the thin line of light under the door went out. He tried the door, and found it unlocked. He threw it open and reached for the switch to the central light of the room. Utter confusion lay in front of him— drawers open, papers strewn about, even the carpet pulled up at the corners. He had scarcely had a moment to take it in when a voice from the bedroom snapped, "Put your hands up and don't move. I've shot better men than you before breakfast."

CHAPTER IX

Ludlow sighed with exasperation and left his hands where they were.

"Come out of there, and stop being a fool," he said.

There was silence for a moment, then a frightened face surmounted by dishevelled red hair peered round the bed-room door. It was Latham.

"You're a poor sort of criminal," said Ludlow. "You can't even disguise your voice. And where do you pick up that ridiculous jargon? I should have thought a man of your age would have grown out of gangster films. Come in here properly and stop looking round that door like a frightened tortoise. Sit down, and explain yourself —if you can."

Latham came in and sat down miserably in the middle of the chaos.

"I didn't know it was you," he said, "that's why I was frightened."

"Indeed? And did you think it unlikely that I should enter my own flat? I should think that the return of the owner would be frightening enough for most people."

"I haven't been here long, not ten minutes."

"You've contrived to make a lot of mess in a short time."

"All this?" Latham gesticulated wildly at the room. "I didn't do that. It was like that when I came—I thought it was normal."

"I own to be notoriously untidy, but I don't live quite like this. So you didn't make this mess, but you still have to explain what you are doing hiding in my bedroom and threatening me with an imaginary gun. That isn't wise, you know—the other man might have a real one."

"I was looking for something."

"For something that you couldn't ask me nicely for in the polite and conventional way? My first edition of *Quentin Durward*—my notes for an article on Webster—some of my rather good dry sherry—I wonder?"

"You're making fun of me."

"If I laugh at any mortal thing, as Byron remarked, 'tis that I may not weep. Or punch your silly nose. You were looking for the papers that Jenny Hexham was so careful to hide."

"How did you know?"

"A lot of people are looking for them, so you're only in the general fashion. What made you think that I have them?"

"Everybody knows that you've been poking around trying to get Robert Trent out of the mess he's in. It's all over the Senior Common Room," he added with malicious satisfaction.

"Is it really? Well, I've never missed a lecture yet for the sake of criminal investigation. But you flatter me in thinking I've been clever enough to get those papers; and when I do they're going straight to the police. Now tell me what interest you have in them."

"That's my business," said Latham sullenly.

"It's public business. This is murder, Latham, no time for private secrets. And by your intrusion here you've made it specially my business as well. By the way, how did you get in here—do you add lock-picking to your other criminal activities? And how did you know I was out for the evening? You'd better talk, Latham, and talk fast. Bother, I'm talking like a gangster-film now; it's very corrupting to the language. Well, get on with it."

"I didn't know you were out. I'd heard that you were following up this case and I thought you might have found the papers——"

"How did you know about the papers anyway?"

"She had told me that she had—well, things I wouldn't like to be seen. I've been in an awful state ever since it happened, wondering what to do. At last I made up my mind to come and see you, to ask if you had the papers and to appeal to you to let me have my—certain things. I came here a few minutes ago. There was no answer when I rang, and I was just going away when I saw that the outer door wasn't quite closed. I pushed it open and went in, and then I started looking around. I thought you might have them somewhere and that I might get hold of them without anybody knowing. When I heard steps outside, I ran into the bedroom. I thought it might be the murderer, after the same thing as I was."

"Very lucky for you that it wasn't." Ludlow moved to the telephone.

"Who are you going to call?"

"Inspector Montero, if he's still at the Yard. If not, any senior officer who knows about the Hexham case."

"You can't do that! I've told you the truth."

"If you have told me the truth, it means that somebody has broken in and searched my flat. In the circumstances, that deserves a call to the police."

Montero was working late at Scotland Yard and agreed to come round when he heard that Ludlow's flat had been entered. Latham, relieved that his name had not been mentioned, made for the door.

"Oh no," said Ludlow, "you're staying here to see the inspector."

"You won't tell him that you found me here?"

"That depends on what you tell me in the next five minutes. What was there among Jenny Hexham's papers that you were so anxious to get your hands on?"

"I'll tell you everything, and trust you not to let me down. The fact is that I got quite—er—friendly with Jenny Hexham. She wasn't one of my own students, of course, but she used to come into the Hall a great deal and I—well, I got friendly with her."

"Do you mean that you had an affair with her?"

"I didn't say that."

"I'm saying it for you. You wouldn't be in such a panic if it wasn't true, and we've no time to waste on euphemisms, which are the curse of the English language anyway. All right—how long did it go on?"

"Last term, about the last six weeks. Then I finished it during the vacation, because I saw where it was leading. You mustn't think too badly of me, Ludlow. She wasn't an innocent girl—she knew quite as much as I did——"

"Probably more. I'm not here as a court of morality. I want to know why you've been so frightened since she was killed and what papers she had that concerned you."

"She didn't like the way I gave her up suddenly. I'd never promised to marry her or anything, and she'd probably have laughed if I had, but she seemed to resent my refusing to have any more to do with her."

"It's not an unusual reaction." Ludlow looked with distaste at his colleague's pale, freckled face. He could well imagine the ineptitude with which Latham would blunder in and out of an affair.

"Well, anyway, she didn't like it. She had some letters

that I had written to her—silly things that one does write —and she wouldn't give them back to me. She kept saying that she'd show me up one day."

"They must have been fairly hot, as I believe the expression goes. And this interesting collection was kept with all the other documents that she was threatening to reveal to a startled world?"

"Yes. She was always boasting about what shocks she could give to a lot of people. She was horrible."

"Apparently you didn't think so a few months ago."

"I didn't know what she was really like. She managed to make me feel sorry for her. She said she looked to me for help and comfort——"

'You poor mug,' thought Ludlow. The doorbell rang so that Latham jumped up.

"Montero," Ludlow said. "He's been remarkably quick."

"You won't tell him anything of what I've just said. Don't you see that he might think it was a motive for murder?"

"Yes, I see that very clearly. What I tell him ultimately depends on what more I discover, but you can sleep soundly for tonight. And if you take my advice, you won't have affairs with students, innocent or otherwise. Keep to a tutorial relationship and forget them once you're outside the college walls."

He opened the door and the caller walked in. It was Sheila Broome. Latham gaped for a long time and then giggled. Ludlow's attempt to recover his composure made him look so severe that Sheila quailed.

"I'm terribly sorry to call on you like this," she said, "but I simply had to know if you'd found out anything today."

"Miss Broome's interest is in Robert Trent," said Ludlow firmly to Latham. "Come and sit down, if you can find anywhere among the mess. I'm just waiting for Inspector Montero. There has been an uninvited visitor, who may or may not have something to do with the business in hand. As to your question, I haven't found Robert but I think I'm pretty near to doing so."

"Oh, I'm so glad!"

Ludlow looked at her with compassion. "You realise," he said, "that finding Robert is not the same thing as proving that he's innocent."

"But you think he is—don't you—or has something happened today to make you doubt it?"

"I'm more sure than ever. But policemen are suspicious people, who want proof. I haven't enough for them yet, though I think I shall in time. The period of waiting may be unpleasant for Robert, but I'm convinced that he's better off and safer with them than where he is now."

"You know where he is then?"

"I'd rather not say any more at the moment. Some people may not share our desire to have this affair cleared up." Latham scowled, then looked at the carpet. There was an uneasy pause.

"I'm awfully glad you were here," said Sheila. "A man followed me all down the street to the flats."

Ludlow sat up. "Where did he come from?" he asked.

"He sort of appeared, at the corner of the street, as if he was—well, just prowling up and down. He walked behind me all the way, till I turned in here. And then he came across the road and watched me go upstairs."

Ludlow sprang to his feet, switched out the light and crossed to the window. The street lights cast a faint glow into the darkened room, making the untidiness look more desolate and giving a green tint to Latham's pale face. A man was standing on the opposite side of the road, looking up at the window of the flat. As the curtain moved, he walked slowly away, looking back over his shoulder after a few yards. It was the man in the shabby raincoat who had been watching Ludlow in the street outside Tanner's house, and later in the Green Man.

"Is that the one who was following you?"

"Yes. Do you know him?"

"Not exactly, but he knows me. He must have made good time from Streatham. I think he's a detective."

"He's not a very good one, if he attracts so much attention to himself," said Sheila.

"That's true. I wonder—well, never mind. He's not doing any harm for the moment." Ludlow drew the curtain across and put on the light again. The three people in the room looked at each other blankly. Nobody knew what to say and each was afraid of saying the wrong thing. Latham was terrified that Ludlow would give him away, and Sheila could sense that she had stumbled on a new mystery. Her wish to help Robert prompted her to ask questions but her awe of the two dons held her silent. Latham fumbled for a cigarette.

"Do you mind if I smoke," he asked ungraciously.

"Not at all, though you certainly smoke too much. You ought to smoke a pipe; it's healthier, and it doesn't stain the fingers."

Latham looked at his brown fingers. He muttered what might have been an apology or a curse, pulled out his cigarette case and offered it to Sheila. She took one, not wanting it but thinking that it would make her look childish to refuse. Her respect for Ludlow was being tempered with the thought that he was getting rather pompous. Ludlow got out his pipe and started to prod and suck at it.

"It doesn't take me all that time to get started," said Latham. "A pipe seems to be more trouble than it's worth. Anyway, I don't smoke very much as a rule."

"Only since last Saturday?" said Ludlow gently.

There was another long pause, while Latham glowered and Ludlow busied himself with the interior of his pipe. Sheila and Latham sat there, each wishing that the other would go so that Ludlow could be consulted on private business.

"The room *is* in a mess," Sheila said at last. "Did you find it like this when you came in?"

"Yes. Mr. Latham happened to be calling about the same time."

"Has anything been stolen?"

"Not as far as I can see. It might be a good idea to make sure, though, while we're waiting."

He prowled about the room humming to himself while Sheila and Latham were reduced to glaring silently at each other through the smoke of their cigarettes. At last a ring at the door broke their agony. Ludlow trotted across the room, and let in Montero. The Inspector seemed surprised to see other people there.

"It's been a busy evening," said Ludlow. "I went out to dinner, and came back about half an hour ago to find the door of the flat unlocked, and all this mess inside. You know my colleague Latham I think—and Miss Broome we were talking of only this morning."

"Yes. Were they with you when you returned?"

"No, I was alone. Latham called just afterwards, and Miss Broome a few minutes later."

"May I ask what you have been doing since you had dinner?"

"I went to a pub and had a few drinks."

"I see. Somebody must have known that your flat was empty. Do you know who it could have been?"

"I've no idea. This is one of those blocks where people live without communicating with each other, so I didn't tell anybody I was going out. I suppose I could have been watched."

"No doubt. Well, whoever it was, he's made a thorough job of it. Is anything missing?"

"Not as far as I can tell—certainly nothing valuable. This time, I've left everything exactly as I found it," he added complacently.

"The wisest thing to do. But I take it that you didn't call me out to report a simple case of breaking and entering. What do *you* think he was after?"

"The same as you and several other people: the papers that Jenny Hexham was so mysterious about."

"Right." Montero seemed to relax at this admission. "I suppose you haven't—or hadn't—got them?"

"No. And I'm no nearer to guessing where they are."

Montero turned to the others. "Did either of you see anybody leaving this building when you arrived?" he asked.

They shook their heads. Montero sat down heavily.

"Well, one thing emerges," he said. "Somebody who's interested in this case knows how to pick a lock—a more difficult one than those at the students' hostel too. That may be important. I'll send a man over later for prints, but I don't suppose we'll get anything. Our man is too clever to do a job without gloves."

"He took a risk, though," said Ludlow, "forcing the door like that."

"Not so much, really, for a man with a cool head. You know what people are like for minding their own business and not wanting to get mixed up in anything—you said yourself that people in these flats don't talk to each other. If they see a man standing outside your door, they won't give him a second glance—you can bet he won't let them actually see him with his instrument in the lock. If anybody speaks to him, he's only got to be a friend calling on you unexpectedly. He'll have made sure where you are, or at any rate that you're not in."

He looked at the others as if expecting one of them to go on where he had stopped. Nobody spoke and he was compelled to do more angling.

"If none of you saw anybody suspicious leaving the building, do you remember any circumstance at all that seemed peculiar? Think hard, because the smallest thing may be of importance."

"There's one thing," said Sheila at once, "a man followed me from the corner of the street right up to the flats."

Montero was on his feet at once and moving to the window, when Ludlow stopped him.

"Tell me something before you look outside," said Ludlow. "Have you had a man watching the Tanners' house in Streatham, where Robert Trent used to lodge."

"Not since yesterday, when this young lady called there. Our inquiries led us to believe that there was nothing to be got there and I moved him. We can't afford to leave men watching all over London when we're three thousand short—and if the papers would stop publicising that fact we might get a little less crime. But why do you ask?"

"Because a man has been watching my movements and seems to have followed me back here. He was across the street a few minutes ago."

Once again the light was put out and the curtains drawn. The shabby man was no longer opposite the flats. He was standing by a car that was parked a little way up the street.

"That's the man," said Ludlow. "Is he one of yours?"

"No, but he's known to us. Wonder how he got pulled into this? If I ring the local station perhaps we can pull him in for loitering with intent and then question him. Damn! He's getting in the car. Too late to get a patrol car after him, and I don't feel like a single-handed chase at this time of night. I'll get his number."

They returned to their seats, a little disappointed that there had been no excitement. Montero alone seemed unperturbed.

"Who is that man?" Ludlow asked.

"I can't remember his real name, and it doesn't matter because it's seldom used. We call him Dirty Charlie."

"For physical or moral reasons?"

"Bit of both. He's a small-time crook who does odd jobs for the big boys and occasionally a bit of informing on the side. I reckon he's been employed to tail you and doesn't know what it's about. We've got enough on him to pick him up any time, but he's useful enough to go free more often than not. That's why I wasn't worried about him getting away now; we know his regular haunts. He probably spotted me coming here and decided it was time to move."

"He's not very good at shadowing people if he gets noticed all the time, is he?" Sheila said.

"No, it's a skilled job to trail a man without being seen

yourself. These fellows aren't trained for it. But Charlie has one asset for a job like this. He's a skilled lip-reader and can pick up a conversation from a distance if necessary."

Ludlow suddenly felt cold. He had thought that his conversation in the Green Man could not possibly have been overheard. If it had the murderer would soon know where Robert was—and might have every reason for seeing that he was not found. He shivered, and Montero as usual missed nothing.

"Well, you've had a busy day, Mr. Ludlow," he said.

"Not terribly," said Ludlow.

"You're too modest about the extent of your activities. After a morning's teaching, and a boring conversation with me, you've been in Streatham, Shepherd's Bush, probably back to Streatham—and come home to find your flat ransacked. That would be enough excitement for most people."

"I didn't say I'd been to Streatham."

"You asked if Dirty Charlie had been there and then said he'd been following you. That's good enough for me."

"Is there any reason why I shouldn't go to Streatham?"

"None at all, so far as I know. But if you co-operate fully with me we'll be a lot nearer to catching the murderer. Which is what we both want—isn't it?" he added in a sharper tone.

"Of course. There isn't much to tell. After I left you this morning, I drove to Streatham and talked to the people at Robert's old lodgings. They could tell me nothing, but suggested I see a young man who was friendly with him. He was at work then of course. I went to see Mrs. Reddle, which you know all about, had dinner and went back to Streatham. I had a drink or two with this boy and came back here to find this mess."

Ludlow hoped that this modified version of the day's activities would get past. Montero seemed satisfied.

"How many times did you see Charlie?" he asked.

"He was watching the Tanners' house this morning— but, of course, he may have followed me from college, guessed where I was making for when I got into the area, and taken a short cut that brought him there before me. He was in the pub this evening. Then he must have followed me back here because he was hanging about when Miss Broome arrived. I didn't see him this afternoon, but he may have kept out of sight."

"We must give him credit for skill with a car, anyway," said Montero. "By the way, what pub were you in this evening?"

"The Green Man, in the High Road."

"Oh yes, I know it. A Mudge's house. The man who built your hostel," he said, turning to Latham. "Not bad stuff. And did you find out anything about our young friend?" he asked Ludlow.

"No." There was no going back on that now. If the other side, whoever they were, knew where Robert was, would it be safer to put the police on him at once? Surely everything depended on finding him first and fitting his story into what had already been learnt. Without that preliminary talk and the voluntary surrender, there might be no hope for him.

"If you do know anything," Montero went on, "you'd do much better to tell me. If the boy's innocent as you believe, no harm can come to him. If he's guilty—well, you wouldn't want to shield him, would you?"

"I've told you all that's come my way. Why should

I lie now?" 'This is the big stuff,' he thought, 'this is getting deeper than I ever intended. In this new world, there's no security in being innocent.' Montero seemed satisfied.

"It doesn't matter," he said. "We're bound to pick him up soon. His description's circulated, but it takes a long time to comb all the pubs and dance-halls and doss-houses in London."

Was it a hint, or a natural way of speaking? Ludlow felt himself sweating. Sheila and Latham seemed to be looking fixedly at him, and Montero's mild blue eyes never left his face.

"You have a pleasantly innocent look about you, Mr. Ludlow," Montero said. "Of course, it could be that you really are innocent." The mouth was smiling but the eyes were cold and hard as ice.

"What exactly does that mean?" asked Ludlow. He tried to sound indignant but his dry tongue produced a choking noise.

"Just what it says. Did you enjoy your little talk with Mrs. Reddle this afternoon?"

"I don't know that enjoy is the right word. It was quite illuminating."

"That's exactly what our man said, only being a simple policeman and not a don he used a shorter word. I must say your skill in interrogation is considerable—or perhaps the public just doesn't trust policemen. Anyway, you found out a couple of things that we hadn't."

"Such as?"

"Such as the fact that Jenny Hexham was frightened of one of her boy-friends who was mixed up with the Communists—frightened to the extent of thinking she might be killed by him. Also that she had been having an affair with one of what Mrs. Reddle described as her teachers."

The room was very still. Sheila gave a little gasp. Latham looked as if he was going to be sick, but Montero's eyes were on Ludlow.

"Robert Trent is, or was, connected with the Communists, if we are to believe a number of apparently reliable witnesses. You think a lot of him, don't you, Mr. Ludlow?"

"He's a very good student and a thoroughly nice young man. I want to get him out of this trouble, which I'm sure is no fault of his."

"Quite so. And by all accounts, he thinks a great deal of you. Of course you have an unbreakable alibi for the time of the murder. But suppose—just let us lightly suppose—that Robert Trent killed Jenny Hexham, motivated by her threats and perhaps by knowledge that she was threatening you too. If you had been indiscreet in your relations with her, you might become very interested in the whereabouts of certain papers she possessed. You might also be anxious to get hold of Trent and talk to him before we did. It's an attractive theory, because it explains a great deal that's otherwise puzzling."

"It explains a great deal that never existed." Anger now had taken the place of fear. "How dare you sit there in my own room and accuse me of such things. You're exceeding your duty——"

"My dear sir, there has been no accusation. I've just been amusing myself with a few passing fancies. I'm deeply sorry if they distressed you in any way. I must be getting along; it's late and you've had a tiring day."

He got up to go. Ludlow became aware of the time; it was just after eleven. Too late to go to the Rosebud that night. Montero noticed his agitation but said nothing of it.

"I'll send a man round in the morning to look for prints," he said. "Try to leave things as they are, so far as it's consistent with your comfort. Can I give either of your friends a lift anywhere?"

Latham looked as if he was afraid that to enter Montero's car would mean being driven straight to prison. However, he accepted and so did Sheila. At the door Montero paused as if something had just occurred to him.

"Tell me one more thing, Mr. Ludlow, if you will. Would it surprise you very much to learn that a witness has come forward who saw a young man running down the road away from Mudge Hall a few minutes after ten-thirty last Saturday evening? A young man who looked wild and frightened, and whose description tallies exactly with the description of Robert Trent. Would that surprise you?"

"No," said Ludlow steadily. "That would not surprise me at all."

"Would it make you feel any doubt about his innocence?"

"No."

"You really ought to be a policeman, Mr. Ludlow. In our job, it's a great advantage never to be surprised by anything. Also to be able to believe what other people find difficult to believe. I've sometimes believed as many as six impossible things before breakfast."

"Have you really, Inspector? Since you're so fond of Lewis Carroll, may I hope that you don't subscribe to the principle of 'sentence first—verdict afterwards'."

Montero smiled very gently. "Neither the sentence no

the verdict is my business," he said. "I'll do my part of the job and leave the rest to others. Which is good advice for people in all professions. Good night."

He shepherded out Sheila and Latham, both bewildered by these last exchanges. Ludlow looked ruefully at his disordered room and went to bed. It was a long time before he slept.

CHAPTER X

The next day passed very slowly for Ludlow, like a day in preparation for battle when there is nothing to do but wait. The first part of the morning was taken up by Montero's emissaries, taking photographs and dusting everywhere for fingerprints. A lecture at twelve o'clock and a leisurely lunch took him a little farther, but still the afternoon stretched in an arid waste before him. On Wednesdays there were no afternoon lectures or classes, the hours being devoted to the cult of sport. Ludlow even thought wildly of going to watch a game, but the idea of so much energy expended under his eyes made him feel tired. He could not hope to find Robert before the Rosebud opened in the evening, and any premature action might lead to action from the very people he did not want to alarm. If they had nothing more to go on than his conversation with Bert in the Green Man, they too would have to wait. If they had done anything the previous evening he would surely have heard of it. At last he threw down the *Review of English Studies* which he was vainly trying to read and drove over to Mudge Hall. If there were any more clues to be picked up, that was the most likely place to find them. Also he was worried by Montero's new attitude—worried less for himself than for Robert. At the Hall, he might run into the Inspector without having to make a formal call. If he could erase the bad impression his searches seemed to have made, it might make things a little easier.

Montero was in fact spending the afternoon at Mudge Hall, accompanied as usual by the faithful Springer. When Ludlow was turning into the Hampstead Road, they had just finished yet another interrogation of Steve and then of Ferris. After the porter had been dismissed, the two officers watched the door close behind him before saying anything. Montero, with a show of impatience that was unusual in him, banged the table with his fist. Springer knew that what his chief really wanted was encouragement to talk over the problem once again.

"Whichever way you look at it, sir," he said, "one of those two is telling lies. And that means that one of them knows more about this case than he wants to let us think."

"I know. And it means that wherever we look we get back to keys. The keys are getting a disproportionate amount of attention. If it wasn't for this discrepancy in their stories, I wouldn't bother so much about how the room was entered."

"It would be a nice solution, sir, if Ferris and Trent were in league over this. When Ferris got the keys back, he gave the master-key to Trent and made up the story about finding them on his desk to throw suspicion elsewhere; Trent had made a big point of giving Jenny his own key and pretending to leave the building."

"And when he got down from the window, he threw the bracelet into the boiler-house for Ferris to pick up as his agreed payment?"

"It would be a nice, neat case if it was like that."

"Unfortunately, this case is neither nice nor neat. It would be a nice, neat case if Ludlow had an interest in Jenny Hexham's death, but I don't see any real evidence that he had."

"You think he's on the level, then?"

"I don't know, Springheels, I really don't know. I think he's found out where Trent is hiding. My impression was that he meant to go after him there last night if he hadn't been held up. I don't know whether he's acting out of decency or out of self-interest—and the line between those two is often so thin that it's a job for a philosopher, not a policeman."

"Do you think he staged that affair in his flat to divert suspicion?"

"Could be—it's an old enough trick, but tests this morning were negative. We may know more when we can have a word with Dirty Charlie." Montero spoke abstractedly. He was looking again at Jenny's gold bracelet which was on the table in front of him.

"Has it occurred to you," he said, "that there's something funny about this story of her keeping the secret of the papers inside her bracelet? Here, look at it again: it's thick and heavy, admittedly, but the surface is quite straight and smooth. If the edges curved inwards there might be more sense in it, but I don't see how anybody could keep a piece of paper in this."

"Not even a railway cloakroom ticket?"

"That's only Ludlow's idea and I don't know where he got it from. He may be trying to put us off the scent."

"It's a possibility, though."

"Yes, but have you any idea how many railway stations there are in the London area, when you include the larger Tube stations? And we have no authority to search all the luggage in them. We may have to get it though, because I've a feeling we shan't have all the evidence we need to pin down this case until we find those papers she was so mysterious about. Here, hold out your wrist."

Springer obeyed, and Montero put the bracelet around the sinewy wrist that was offered to him. By pressing hard, it was just possible to snap it shut. Springer looked on with interest.

"I thought you'd found me out and were going to put the 'cuffs on me, sir," he said.

"Don't worry, I shan't turn you in till this case is solved. Now do you see what's in my mind?"

"It suits me, doesn't it? A bit tight though."

"Tight, but it just clasps. Now, if it will clasp on your great hairy wrist, it must have been fairly loose on hers— the sort that slides about but won't quite slip off over the hand. How was she going to keep anything inside that?"

"She might have stuck it in with a bit of adhesive," said Springer, removing the bracelet.

"It would be a pretty insecure way of keeping something that she thought worth making a mystery about. I think she had them all fooled, and the secret was somewhere else."

"Which leaves us exactly where we were at the beginning."

"Not quite. When you've eliminated one false trail, you're that much better off. But I don't think we're going to get a lot farther until we find Trent. He may be guilty, and if he isn't he can probably put us on to the one who is."

It was at this point in their deliberations that Ludlow put his head round the door and asked if Montero could spare him a few minutes. To his surprise, the Inspector received him very cordially.

"I just wondered if you knew who had broken into my flat," said Ludlow.

"Well, Mr. Ludlow, I'll admit to you that we haven't

much to go on so far. But we've traced the car that Dirty Charlie was using. It came from a hire-firm in the West End. It was ordered by phone for a week, by a man who gave his name as Smith. From his voice, it wasn't Charlie. But Charlie picked it up the day before yesterday, and paid cash in advance. The car was found abandoned near Euston this morning."

"Have you talked to this Charlie yet?"

"No, but we will in our own time."

"Euston. And Quantrough lives near King's Cross. Had that occurred to you?"

"It had, sir. We're not such fools as some people seem to think. We had a word with Quantrough today before coming here. He denies any association with Dirty Charlie, or with Communists. He repeated his story that Jenny Hexham owed him money for books, and showed us copies of invoices."

"A man can easily fake invoices."

"I fully realise that."

"Did he admit that I had called on him on Monday?"

"It was more of an attack than an admission. He said you'd come there pestering and accusing him of Communist sympathies. He seemed to think you were a crank, possibly harmless and possibly not, and advised me to keep on eye on you."

"Do you believe me or him?"

Montero only smiled.

"If you won't tell me that, I'll ask you something else. Are you going to arrest Robert when you find him?"

"If you read the papers carefully, you'd see that we want him for questioning in connection with our inquiries into the death of Jenny Hexham. Whether he is charged after questioning depends on what sort of story he has, and the state of the case when we find him. There, Mr. Ludlow, I've been frank with you. I'll hope you'll always be as frank with me."

"I'll tell you this much, but perhaps you know this too. Jenny Hexham was becoming disillusioned with Communism and was near to leaving the Party. You probably have a note from your man that Mrs. Reddle told me that, but I have it from another source too."

"You'd like me to conclude from that—well, what exactly?"

"Robert regretted his associations with the Communist Party too. He had nothing to fear from her if he felt the same way."

"I'll want more substantial evidence first. Besides, he may have had other reasons that we don't know about—yet."

The two men stood for a moment, each trying to understand and weigh up what the other was really thinking. Montero had been trained in a hard school, and it was Ludlow who at last turned away and made an excuse to go. After he had left, Springer patted his notebook affectionately.

"That one's getting nervous," he said. "I think he's going to be worth watching. Shall I put a man on him, sir?"

Montero shook his head. "Not yet. If we haven't found Trent soon, perhaps I will. But I've got a feeling that we're not far off getting him."

"One of your hunches, sir?"

"Yes. But our work won't be finished then. If Trent is the actual murderer, there's at least one man who knows more about the case than is healthy for him. I mean the one who called at the girl's lodgings the day after she was killed. Even though he was disguised, it was a much bigger man than Trent."

"About the size of our friend Quantrough."

"Yes, but I doubt whether Quantrough would have gone back in his own person with another story when he'd already failed in disguise. And did you look at his fingers? There were no tobacco stains on them."

"And it seems that Robert Trent's vices don't include smoking. Looks as if we're scrambling, sir."

Ludlow somehow got through the rest of the day. He knew that it would be unwise to go to the Rosebud very early in the evening. In the middle of the week the attendance was likely to be small, and he needed a crowd if he was to work unobtrusively. He sighed as he thought how long it was since he had been to a dance of any kind, and he wondered how these modern dance-halls were run. Bert and Lorna had seemed decent enough, but Bert's assessment of the working conditions had not been at all encouraging. It was probable that large men were employed to eject people who made any trouble. If it was so hard to get waiters, the management would resent any attempt to remove one during working hours. And suppose Robert would not come with him? His tutorial authority and influence would be wearing very thin in this world of murder and suspicion. And suppose the lad was guilty after all? Ludlow decided that he was not looking forward to the evening. He tried to close his mind to the immediate future and used some of his bachelor skill in cooking himself a meal. He also cut a lot of sandwiches and prepared things for coffee.

At nine o'clock he left his flat, carefully checking that the door was locked and went downstairs. Outside the general entrance, a figure edged itself out of a shadow and seized his arm. It was the man that Montero had called Dirty Charlie. A hoarse voice whispered:

"You keep out of this, mate. You've gone far enough. If you don't want to get hurt, start minding your own business, quick."

Ludlow wondered whether to try to hold the man and take him to the police. He doubted his ability to do so, and he certainly could not afford to waste another evening. If he called up Montero again, Robert would still be in danger. He shook the man's hand away and walked off to where Cleopatra was parked down the road. As soon as he had gone, another, larger figure appeared from what had seemed to be an empty doorway. The new-comer took Charlie in a practised grip.

"Come along, Charlie," he said. "Inspector Montero would like to have a little chat with you."

CHAPTER XI

In spite of its name, the Rosebud gave the impression of being overblown rather than blooming. It peeled its pre-war façade of grandeur in all directions, the flaking outer walls a contrast to the sheen which modern plastics were able to give to the entrance. A pink outline of a rosebud flickered in uncertain neon above the door, and green lights had spelt the word "Dancing" until the C went out and left a vague suggestion of Scandinavia. A door-man hitched his padded shoulders in a cool autumn evening and regarded Ludlow with a look of amazement that was wrongly interpreted as hostility. Certainly Ludlow's rough tweed suit was a visitation from another planet in comparison with the cheap elegance that usually passed that way, and his heavy brogues gave no promise of dancing. He was relieved to find a familiar type of cash desk that might have stood in the foyer of any cinema, and as the price of admission was plainly marked he was able to get by without any show of his ignorance. The doorman tore his ticket and reminded him to get a pass if he went out and wanted to return. Thinking that the last thing he wanted to do was to return to this place once his task was accomplished, Ludlow walked through the inner door which again held out the promise of "Dancing". The announcement was hardly necessary, for a persistent wail underlying a swishing noise from inside left no room for doubt.

Ludlow was not quite sure what he expected to see. His brushes with the criminal world in the last few days had left him desperately ready to enter an Imperial orgy or an opium den if he could only bring to an end his self-imposed quest. What he did see, as he stood at the top of a short flight of steps, was a room that was too low-ceilinged for comfort, filled with an assortment of young people. 'If this is a quiet night, thank goodness I didn't come at a week-end,' he thought. The walls were lined with chairs on three sides of the room and the chairs were lined with girls trying to look as if they hadn't come to dance and much preferred to watch. The other wall was taken up by tables in a space railed off from the dance-floor, at the back of which there was a bar. Crammed into one corner, on a dais so small that they seemed to be in danger of elbowing each other off with each note, five men blew or strummed or banged according to their several vocations. Four of them wore blue jackets with pink rosebuds embroidered on the breast-pockets. The fifth, whose jacket was entirely pink, was presumably the famous Lew Tatters himself. What surprised Ludlow most was the dancers. They moved with a fierce dedication, seldom smiling or speaking, twisting and gyrating with faces as set as if they were performing some ritual of a penitential nature. The dancing was quite unlike anything he remembered from his younger days and seemed at first to be without form or pattern; but as he watched it with the fascination of the unknown, a certain grace began to emerge. This was an expression of something that he had never stumbled on in his researches.

Realising that he was doing the very thing he wanted to avoid and making himself conspicuous, he trotted down the stairs and sat on the nearest vacant chair. Most of the people around him were very young, but to his relief they seemed to take little notice of him—or indeed of each other. All eyes were turned hypnotically on the dancing. There were also enough older men to make him feel a little more comfortable, though he began to think of the incongruity of his clothes and especially of his shoes. 'Still,' he thought, 'being a man I won't be asked to dance—or can one even be sure of that with these young women?' He forced himself to sit quietly and not to look in the direction of the bar. An old wartime voice came back, instructing him, 'Fade into your surroundings.' Which was not going to be so easy in surroundings like these. He forced himself to look straight ahead until he realised that he was staring fixedly at a girl with magenta lips who was standing on the edge of the dance-floor. She neither turned away nor smiled, but returned his stare with sullen appraisal. The band, which had been going on as if actuated by some principle of perpetual motion, fell silent with a roll on the drum. There was a little sporadic clapping and a few couples drifted off the floor but the majority stood where they were and looked hopefully at Lew Tatters and his associates. However, there was enough movement to make it possible to explore without being too conspicuous and Ludlow moved to a position where he could get a good view of the bar.

Several of the tables were occupied but the biggest crowd was around the bar itself. Two men in short white coats moved between the tables and a corner of the bar that bore the sign, "Waiters Only". One of them was tall and thin, with fair hair that rose to a peak in front. The other was elderly and bald. There was no sign of Robert. Ludlow wondered whether all that had happened so far had been wasted. He remembered that Bert had no known whether Robert had found or even looked for a job in this place, only that it had been vaguely discussed. If he were not here, all the week had gone for nothing and he had to start again with the known lines of inquiry exhausted. The band started to make encouraging noises again and Ludlow returned to the wall before worse befell him. He found that he was sitting next to a woman whose face was younger than her neck and who regarded him with an interest that he found flattering. After a while she produced a cigarette case and held a cigarette plaintively in the air for a long time. As he did not respond to this, she was reduced to asking him openly for a light, which he gave her. He also accepted one of her cigarettes though he had no liking for them in the ordinary way. But he was beginning to understand the nervous state that could make people chain-smokers. The woman watched him through the smoke, under eyelids lowered in the approved manner.

"Good band, isn't it?" she said at last.

"Is it? I mean, yes, I'm sure it is. It's not the kind of music I know much about."

"Do you come here often?"

"No."

"Thought I hadn't seen you here before. Do you like dancing?"

"No."

"Wouldn't you like to dance now?"

"No—er—thank you," he added, realising that it was an invitation rather than a question.

"Maybe you didn't come here to dance?"

"No, I didn't."

"I don't care so much about dancing either. Shall we go for a little walk?"

"No, I think I'd rather stay here."

"What about a little drink then?"

Ludlow thought that this might be a good idea but he had no intention of saddling himself with this woman for the rest of the evening.

"The fact is, madam," he said with severity, "I am looking for a young friend who may be here."

This did not discourage her but brought a new flood of interest and sympathy.

"Hasn't she turned up, dear? Or has she come here with somebody else? That's bad luck, but don't worry, it'll be all the same tomorrow. You'll forget her, dear, like all the rest. Now what do you say, you and me go and have a little drink?"

"No, no, you don't understand one word I'm saying. It's a student of mine who's in trouble—oh bother!"

He got up and strode away across the floor, to the ruination of several stockings and bruising of a number of small shoulders that rebounded from his bony frame. 'I'm not much of a detective,' he thought furiously. 'I'm hopeless. I'm useless. Probably that woman will come after me and have me thrown out. Or she'll go to the police. Oh dear!'

He need not have worried, for stranger encounters had passed many times in the Rosebud and would pass many times again. It had the good effect, however, of moving him to action. He found himself across the floor and approaching the bar. There was still no sign of Robert, though the two waiters were scurrying to and fro. He attached himself to a comparatively empty part of the bar and waited for a long time. At last the bored woman behind it moved in his direction and gave a silent jerk of her head that was clearly meant to invite his order.

"A whisky and soda, please—better make it a double."

"Soft drinks only here," she snapped.

"Oh. Well, I'd better have some lemonade."

'I wonder how many solecisms you have to commit in this place before they throw you out?' he thought. 'And fancy these young people showing so much energy on lemonade.' Thus meditating on the brave new world, he sipped the glass of fizzy liquid that was put before him and considered his campaign. He did not feel inclined to try any conversation with the woman behind the bar. He wondered whether it would be any good asking for the manager, but decided that it would be wise not to draw any more attention to himself than he could help. A new thought came to him and, leaving his lemonade on the bar, he went and sat at one of the tables. After he had made a few hopeful gestures, the thin fair youth approached and was asked to bring him some lemonade. When this at last arrived, Ludlow placed a half-crown on the tray and told him to keep the change. Bert's pessimistic view of the level of tipping at the Rosebud was obviously right, for the waiter's jaw dropped and he looked almost frightened.

"I'd like to ask you something," said Ludlow. "Here, have a seat."

"Can't do that. Not allowed to stand around talking to customers—nor sitting neither."

"Well, just tell me this. Is there a young man called Robert Trent working here as a waiter?"

"No."

"A pity. He's an old friend of mine and somebody told me he had a job here. I've only got a few hours in London, and I thought I might get a chance of a word with him."

"Never heard of him."

"Aren't there any other waiters here except you and the chap over there?"

"There's Tony."

"What's his other name?"

"Don't know."

"Where is he now?"

"Looking after Mr. Eddy—that's the manager. He often has a few friends in the office about now—regular customers like—and one of us takes in the drinks. It's Tony's turn tonight."

"But he'll be back here later?"

"Any time now."

"How long has Tony been working here?"

"Started on Monday. I got to go."

He went. Ludlow sat back and drank some more lemonade. This seemed to be his last chance. A few minutes later another white-coated figure emerged from a door near the band. It was a rather short young man, pale and ill-looking. He had fair hair, and Robert Trent's hair was dark. He wore glasses and Robert did not. But Ludlow knew at once that his search was over.

The young man went to the bar and spoke to the elderly waiter. Then he started to walk among the tables. When he came near, Ludlow said in a low, clear voice, "Come here, Robert." The youth froze, looked as if he was about to run, and then all his defences broke. He staggered rather than walked towards the table.

"Mr. Ludlow, what are you doing here?"

"Looking for you, Robert. Come and talk to me."

"I'm not allowed to do that, sir."

"Well, bring me some more of this repulsive lemonade if you want an excuse."

When Robert came back, Ludlow took his arm and spoke urgently.

"You've got to get away from here. There are people who know that you're here, and the police may know too at any time. My car's outside."

"Mr. Ludlow, I didn't do it. I didn't kill her."

"I know you didn't, and that's why I've spent all this week looking for you. But you're going to find it hard to convince the police of that unless we move quickly."

"You're not going to give me up to the police?"

"No, you're going to give yourself up to them."

"I can't, I daren't. Haven't you seen the papers—how they want to question me? You know what that means. They think I did it."

"You and I together will convince them of their error. The Inspector in charge of the case is apt to jump to conclusions on inadequate reasoning. That is the inevitable result of not having an academic training. But he is not an unintelligent man, and surprisingly well-read."

"But I can't just put myself in their hands like that. I'm afraid, terribly afraid."

"Listen to me, Robert. Have I given you any reason to distrust me while I've been your tutor?"

"No, sir. I've always told people how good you've been and how much you've taught me. But this is something different."

"Is it? This isn't so far removed from some of those texts we've discussed together. Life is the raw material of literature—but no time for that now. Will you believe me that the best hope you've got is to leave this place now and let me handle what comes after?"

"Just walk out, now?"

"Yes. They can't stop you. But it might be as well not

to use the main door. Is there any way we can slip out and get back quietly to the street."

"There's an emergency exit over there, by the bar. I'll go through that and you can follow me. If we wait till there's a popular dance, no one is likely to notice us."

"All the dances look equally popular to me. I'd rather we moved now."

"All right. Turn left when you get outside and you'll be back on the street where you came in. I'll go now."

Robert walked away, ignoring frantic appeals from some of the tables. He went past the bar and picked up a crate of empty bottles as he did so. With his shoulder he pushed open a door that showed only darkness beyond it. The next two minutes were the longest that Ludlow had ever lived. At last he got up and walked in the way that Robert had gone. Nobody stopped him when he opened the door and stepped through. For a moment everything seemed to be quite dark, after the light of the hall. Then as he grew accustomed to it, he saw that he was in a narrow passage facing a blank wall. To his right there was another wall with crates and dustbins piled against it. From the left, the glow of the street gave what little light there was. Outlined against it, Robert was struggling with two men. His white coat showed up in the gloom. Ludlow ran towards him, and saw as he did so that one of the men was Quantrough. The other was a burly, nondescript man, who seemed to be doing most of the work and had reduced Robert to breathless silence. With a speed that surprised him whenever he thought about it afterwards, Ludlow rushed at Quantrough and hit him. The blow was aimed at the face, but Quantrough turned in time and Ludlow's fist jarred on his shoulder. The two men grappled. Ludlow had no idea of how to defend himself and an arm that seemed as hard as iron tightened round his neck. He kicked feebly and heard a sharp oath, but his strength was rapidly fading. The dim light of the alley seemed to have turned to a suffused redness. He had a vague impression that the ground was sinking and turning to mud. There was a sound like waves, underlying a rapid slapping noise. Then a woman started screaming very loudly.

The pressure on his throat relaxed a little and with a last effort he broke free. Turning, he found himself face to face with Sheila Broome, who was busy hitting Quantrough with her handbag. The burly man dropped Robert, who was obviously incapable of any further fight, and caught her from behind. Ludlow somehow parried a fresh attack from Quantrough and hit out again. This time his fist went where he had intended and his opponent fell back clutching his nose. Before the attack could be followed up, the burly man flung Sheila from him so that she fell sprawling on the ground and came at Ludlow. The blow that he aimed would have been a vicious one if it had connected fully, but Ludlow dodged and got only a glancing tap on the side of his head. That was enough to throw him off his balance, however, just as Quantrough returned to the fight and dragged him down. He lay on his back, waiting for the foot which rose above him to descend, and feeling surprisingly objective about it. The foot faltered, kicked upwards and disappeared from view. Cautiously stretching his neck, Ludlow saw that another man had joined the fight, a big man in a duffle coat who appeared to be on the right side. At all events, it was now Quantrough's turn to be on the ground, and the burly man who was with him was holding his stomach. Robert was beginning to get up, and Sheila's screams were penetrating. Quantrough got up and decided that things were getting too hot. He ran shakily to the end of the alley and disappeared, closely followed by his associate.

Ludlow felt comfortable and disinclined to get up. He lazily watched his new ally helping Sheila to her feet. She at once went over to Robert, who was leaning against the wall and getting his breath back in gulps. The man in the duffle coat came over, and Ludlow found himself looking up into the glasses and inquiring eyes of Henry Prentice. He suddenly realised that it was time to move and move quickly. He leaned for a moment on the offered arm, and they both looked at Sheila and Robert.

"I seem to have done my little bit," said Prentice gently. "I had better fade away now."

"We'd all better fade away," said Ludlow, taking charge again. "Come on, you two. My car's just down the road and we'll leave explanations until later. I can't understand why they're not pouring out of that place after us already."

"You soon learn not to take any notice of a few screams in this place," said Robert.

The side door of the Rosebud had in fact opened, and the elderly waiter was regarding them all with detached interest. Other figures appeared behind him and there was a general movement into the alley. Ludlow led the way to the street. There was no sign of Quantrough and his friend, and the front of the dance-hall seemed quiet. They hurried to the turning down which Ludlow had parked Cleopatra, and piled in. He pulled the old-fashioned starter and produced only a discouraging whir. After several attempts he got out, comforting himself with the thought that the starting-handle would make a useful weapon if necessary. On the third turn, the engine woke up, coughed, and expressed its willingness to turn the wheels. They turned back into the main street just as two police cars rushed past and screamed to a stop outside the Rosebud. A little crowd of uniformed figures ran into the entrance while two disappeared down the side alley. Ludlow got into top gear and headed north.

CHAPTER XII

Nobody spoke until they were past Warren Street station. Then Ludlow eased his foot back a little and said:

"Where do you live, Miss Broome?"

"In St. John's Wood. But don't worry about me. I'd much rather stay and see how things go."

"I'll drop you there and then take Mr. Prentice a little nearer to his hostel. I won't go right up to it. Then I can take a long way back to my flat. If I drive slowly now there's no reason why we should attract any attention. Inspector Montero knows the number of this car, but that's a risk we have to take. He may not know that I was at that place. But the sooner we split up the better. There's no reason for you two to be involved any more than you are."

"What do you want me to do?" Robert asked.

"Stay with me until we've talked things over. You'll have to go to the police, but if you go voluntarily and prepared for the questions they'll ask you, you'll stand a much better chance of convincing them. The other two had better not mention this evening's bit of excitement to anybody for the time being."

"I won't breathe a word," said Sheila.

"You can count on me," said Prentice.

"I'd rather like to know how the two of you came to be in that place this evening. I expect you'd like to know how I came to be there as well, but that piece of

164

curiosity had better go unsatisfied for tonight at least. Also the identity of our attackers. Let it suffice to say that I was not there by chance, and not for any love of what went on there—dancing or whatever they call it. You must try to explain to me one day what possible pleasure you get from these gyrations, in a fetid atmosphere and a blaring noise. It may be a sign of the tendency towards primitivism in the arts, though there is scarcely enough sense of community—however, that can wait."

He glanced at Henry Prentice who was sitting next to him and looking rather embarrassed.

"It's a good thing you came when you did, Prentice," he said. "Did you know that we were there?"

"Not that you and Robert were, sir. I followed Sheila." He looked more embarrassed than ever, and twisted apologetically towards the couple in the back seat. "I'm sorry, and you must think it cheek of me. But I've been afraid all the time you'd get into some trouble if you went looking for Robert. I hung round your digs and followed you into that place. I didn't see Robert—I wouldn't have recognised him anyway in that disguise. I did see Mr. Ludlow, but didn't connect him—I mean I thought he'd just come to dance."

Ludlow snorted and again lifted his eyes from the road to look at Prentice, but saw only a bland, innocent expression.

"I didn't realise what it all meant until the last minute," Prentice went on. "When you went out, I followed you and you went round to the alley at the side and—well, there it was."

"Lucky for us too," said Robert. "I was too winded to do anything, and Mr. Ludlow had just passed out."

"I was having a rest before further combat," Ludlow said, "but I was certainly glad of some help. You must be able to hit very hard."

"I just hit out. I surprised myself, really."

"I helped too, didn't I?" said Sheila. "I mean I screamed and hit him with my handbag."

"You did jolly well," Prentice said. "Are you all right now?"

"I'm fine."

"It was seeing you on the ground more than anything else that put fight into me. Well, now Robert's back I promise I shan't hang around any more. I'm glad, though, that I've been able to let you know how I felt."

"You've been very sweet," said Sheila.

"But how did you come to go there yourself?"

"Robert sent for me."

Ludlow, who had been listening to all this with silent interest, jerked his head round so that Cleopatra nearly mounted the kerb.

"When did he do that?" he asked.

"I had a letter from him this morning. He said where he was working and asked me to go and tell him everything that was going on. And he said he'd dyed his hair and was wearing glasses, and was called Tony. I watched the bar for a long time and then when he appeared Mr. Ludlow got hold of him. I saw them go out, and I ran round by the front way. I knew about that side door and that they could only get round into the street. When I got there, Robert was on the ground and another man was killing Mr. Ludlow."

"It wasn't as bad as that," Ludlow said crossly. "I was defending myself vigorously and I appear to have survived. Never mind. We are now in the region known as St. John's Wood. I should welcome some further directions."

He was given directions, and both Sheila and Prentice were dropped at suitable points. Robert began to speak his thanks.

"I want no thanks or explanations until we are more able to express ourselves rationally," said Ludlow. "We are both badly in need of food and drink, and no man can overcome those needs by thought alone. At least I can't."

They drove in silence to Ludlow's flat. He was half expecting to find either police or criminals waiting for him and was by no means sure which would be the least welcome. However, they were able to go upstairs unmolested and were soon eating sandwiches and drinking coffee laced with some excellent brandy. Robert, still in his waiter's white coat and considerably the worse for the strain of the last few days, began to look more cheerful and again tried to thank Ludlow.

"Don't thank me yet, because it remains to be seen whether we are fully out of our difficulties. We have certainly come a long way."

Robert moved anxiously in his chair. "Do you think Sheila will be all right, sir?" he asked.

"That young woman is quite capable of looking after herself—and looking after you too, by the look of things. And you needn't worry about Prentice. He could see quite clearly how things were."

"Oh, I'm not. Henry is a jolly good chap."

"He certainly made himself felt tonight, in more ways than one. However. Now, there are a lot of things that you've got to tell me. First, perhaps you'll explain in words of one syllable why you ran away. Also why, having run away, you didn't immediately get in touch with me instead of that very nice but inevitably immature girl. I've had the devil of a job finding you."

Robert looked surprised. "But I couldn't bother you with all that," he said. "It wouldn't have been right to bring you into it, and anyway I never thought for a moment that you were interested. I mean, you've been a wonderful tutor, but this wasn't anything to do with work."

Ludlow sat for two or three minutes without speaking. He wondered when things had started going wrong, when students and tutors had come to think of their relationship only as one of formal instruction. Was it since the war, when the university population expanded and the old contacts of reading-parties and leisurely evenings broke down? Or had it always existed, and was this just another page in the long history of how human beings tried and failed to make real communication? He roused himself at last and resumed his brusque manner.

"Before we go any further," he said, "I want you to tell me briefly all that has happened to you since Jenny Hexham arrived at your room last Saturday evening. Let me say again that I know you did not murder her. But the case against you looks bad to some people, and you may be able to give me what I need to convince them of the truth. Also there are people who know quite well that you are innocent but who want to keep you out of the way. We've had proof of that tonight. Now, begin at the beginning, go on till you come to an end, and then stop, as the King said to the White Rabbit."

"Last Saturday—yes, it is only as long as that, isn't it, but it feels as if I've lived through years since then. Jenny came to see me about half past eight."

"Were you expecting her?"

"Not for certain, but she said she might look round. We'd been seeing quite a lot of each other."

"I must ask you this, because it's bound to come out sooner or later. What exactly were your relations with her?"

"Well—there wasn't anything in them. I mean nothing, well—er—physical. I wasn't her type at all. She liked older men, or men with money who could give her a good time. Though she wasn't nearly as bad as some people would make out. Fundamentally, she was rather a serious girl and she knew an awful lot about politics and modern history and things like that. You probably know I've been having a sort of Communist phase. Well, that's how I got friendly with Jenny. Actually, I've always been rather keen on Sheila, but I've been neglecting her badly lately. I'm going to stick to her now."

"I doubt whether she will give you any option. However, yes—Jenny. Now am I right in saying that you had become somewhat, shall we say disillusioned, about Communism, and that she was putting pressure on you to continue your activities?"

"When I said I didn't want to stay in the Party—that was at the beginning of this term—she hinted that I would be unwise to give it up. She said she had enough to get me into trouble if I tried to get away. It had me scared for a bit, but she didn't press it very hard and I soon realised there was nothing in it. After all, Communism isn't illegal in this country, and I certainly hadn't done anything for them that was against any sort of law. I'd only been to a few meetings and parties. Jenny liked to put the wind up people like that—she was always saying that one day she'd surprise an awful lot of people. I don't think she meant it."

"One person at least clearly thought that she did. This all referred to her famous collection of papers that she made so much mystery about?"

"Yes. Have they been found?"

"No, but they'll have to be before this business can be cleared up. I'll want to know more about that later, but now just go on with your story. What happened after she arrived on Saturday?"

"We just sat in my room and talked."

"Was she still threatening you?"

"Oh no. In fact she told me that she was going to leave the Party pretty soon. She'd been doing a lot of thinking, and she'd come to see that most of them had no idea of what the whole thing really meant. Those who did, had quite different intentions from those they put out publicly. She told me, because she knew I was fed up with them and had been rather worried. She wasn't a bad-hearted girl at all, but she liked to make mysteries and feel important."

"What did she intend to do with those papers of hers?"

"She didn't say anything about it."

"So you talked quite amicably that evening. For how long?"

"Until about quarter past nine. Then we just hadn't got any more to say to each other and it was obvious she was bored. She said she'd just go and look about the Hall and see who was in. She was like that, didn't mind wandering about the place and dropping in on anybody she happened to know. So I said she'd better leave her things in my room and take the key, so that she'd have somewhere to come back to and sit if she didn't find anybody."

"You must have been feeling well-disposed towards her."

"Well, it was certainly a relief to know that she was giving up the Communists. I felt that left the way quite clear for me and that I didn't have to worry any more. I told her to leave the key in the door if she came back and found nobody there, because I might go out. Actually, I went down to see Henry Prentice. He lives on the floor below, and I knew he'd be in because he hardly ever goes out in the evenings. He's terribly brainy, and ambitious too. I think he'll make quite a name."

"Are you a close friend of his?"

"Not really, but he's very easy to talk to and he can often give you good advice. I felt like a chat with somebody, so I went to his room. He was there, and we sat and talked."

"What did you talk about?"

"Oh—things."

"About Jenny perhaps—or Sheila?"

"No. I said Jenny had been with me and had gone prowling off and he laughed. We didn't say anything about Sheila. I didn't know that he was at all keen on her. That must have blown up rather suddenly. I hope it's going to be all right; I mean, I've been an awful fool to neglect her for so long. Anyway, about five to ten, I thought it was time I made a move and left him to get on with his work, so I said I'd slip out before the front door was shut and go over to the dance at college. That went on until eleven. He said that was a good idea, and I went."

"To the dance?"

"No, I mean I went out of his room. I intended to go to the dance, and I went downstairs to look at the weather.

It was raining, but it hadn't sounded too bad in my room or Henry's. We're on the back——"

"And the wind was blowing the rain hard against the other side of the building." Seeing Robert's look of surprise, Ludlow went on, "Of course, you didn't know that I was there that evening. With the Warden. Yes, I was well aware of the direction of the wind. Go on."

"The stairs come out at the back of the main hall, to the left of the porter's desk and behind it, and there's another flight down to the basement and courtyard. I went down, and as soon as I stepped into the open, I realised what a frightful night it was. I decided there and then not to go out. Just as I got back into the hall, I saw Desai—he's an Indian student. One of us, I forget which, suggested a game of table-tennis, so we went back to the basement and played for about half an hour. At half past ten I began to think I'd been a bit of a fool to leave Jenny alone. I mean, she was quite capable of settling down in somebody's room and forgetting about the time. As I'd signed her in, I'd have to carry the can if Ferris didn't get her signed out by the official time for guests to leave. So I told Desai, and we stopped playing, and I went up to my room to see if she'd gone."

"Are you sure you didn't go because you'd arranged for her to be there, and knew you'd find her there at that time?"

"No, really, I only hoped she'd gone. I had no idea what—what I was going to find." His voice faltered.

Ludlow got up and went to the window. He looked down into the street before he spoke again. Everything was very quiet. It was a street where there was never much traffic, and only the steady roar from the main road suggested that they were in London and not in some remote country town. Tonight there seemed to be no watchers below. He did not look at Robert until he had said what needed to be said.

"I believe you. But that is the sort of question that Inspector Montero will ask you, and I want you to be prepared for it. Now I know that the next part of what you have to tell me is very painful, and something that you would much rather forget. I hope it will not be long before you can forget it, but now it is important for you to remember it, every detail. Go on from the point where you left Desai."

"I went upstairs." Robert's voice was quite steady now. "The key was in my door, and I thought that she'd gone and left it there for me as we arranged. I turned it and tried to open the door to go in. It stuck, as if there was something pressing against it. I thought I heard somebody moving inside, and supposed it was her."

"Did you call to her?"

"No. I was afraid Mr. Latham was about and would hear. I just pushed hard at the door, and eventually it opened and something fell over. I went in and—I don't want to remember."

"You must, for your own sake."

"I don't know why I was sure at once that she was dead. Her face was swollen, and her tongue was sticking out. I couldn't believe it. Her handbag was lying on the floor, with things spilt all over the rug. I just stood there and looked at her."

Ludlow turned from the window and went and put his hand on the boy's shoulder. When he asked his next question he tried to keep the urgency out of his voice.

"Did you take your own key out of the door when you went in?"

"I suppose I must have, because I found the key in my pocket later. I think I remember pushing the door shut behind me. I don't know how long I was there—it was like a nightmare when you can't run away. The next thing I can remember is Mr. Latham's voice telling me to open the door. Then I just panicked."

"Why? Wasn't it the right thing to open the door and let him take charge?"

"I suppose it was, but I was too scared."

"What did you have to fear?"

"Being there, with her dead on the floor, in my own room. How could they fail to think that I'd killed her? I'd told plenty of people that we disagreed about things —and they didn't know she was leaving the Party and that I had no more to fear from her."

"Nevertheless, was it the action of an innocent man to run away?" Robert got up and walked across the room. He turned with his back to the door and looked hopelessly at Ludlow.

"I'm sorry, Mr. Ludlow, if you don't believe me. I thought you were on my side. I can see how it looks to you, but I've told you the truth. I was just terribly frightened, and as things went on it became more and more impossible for me to go back. I'll leave now, and not give you any more trouble."

"Sit down, Robert," Ludlow said quietly, "and stop behaving like an idiot. I've told you more than once that I believe you, but you have to get used to these questions. You'll be asked worse than that before you've finished. Now where were we? You had just heard Mr. Latham telling you to open the door. What did you do then?"

"I ran over to the window. It was wide open and the

fire-escape thing had been unfastened. I hadn't really noticed it before, but that seemed to be the way for me to get out. I just got hold of the sling arrangement that goes round your shoulders, and let myself go hanging on to it. I'd done it more than once in fire-practice so it didn't worry me."

"Now think carefully again. One end of the apparatus was hanging loose in the window. What about the other end?"

"That was already dangling down outside. I noticed that just as I let myself go."

"Was it right down to the ground?"

"I can't be sure how far it had gone. It was hanging loose, and the other end came up past me as I went down. As soon as my feet touched the ground, I let go and ran."

"Back into the building?"

"No, that would have been no good because the front door can't be opened from inside after Ferris has locked it with the special key at ten. I ran across the courtyard and climbed the wall into the street."

"That's quite a climb, isn't it? The courtyard is below street level, so you have a double distance to go, as it were."

"It's a high wall, but it's so worn that it's easy to get holds on it and then just drop over from the top. We often use it if we want to get in or out after time—I mean, some of the chaps do."

"Now I put it to you that your story of coming down the fire-escape is true, but that you did not leave the courtyard over the wall. You used the other way that is well known to students and went through the boiler-house and up the coke-shoot into the street in front of the building.

In doing so, you dropped the gold bracelet which you had taken from Jenny Hexham's wrist and in your haste were afraid to go back for it. In fact it fell among the coke where it was found next day, and it is now in the possession of the police."

Ludlow looked very grave as he spoke. Robert leapt up and went pale. Then he laughed and sat down again.

"I realise that you're just testing me," he said. "But whoever asks me, the answer is the same. I went over the wall, and I didn't have her bracelet." He frowned thoughtfully. "As a matter of fact, I don't think it was on her wrist when I—found her. Everything is so muddled that I can't be sure. I am sure that she had it earlier in the evening."

"All right. Go on with your story."

"I just ran, I don't know for how long. I was terrified, and all the time her face was dancing about in front of me, as I'd just seen it. It was pouring with rain, but I didn't seem to notice that at the time. At last I just had to stop. I'd no idea where I was, but I found in the morning that I'd run to somewhere in Chalk Farm. By stumbling about I found myself in the garden of a big empty house—it looked as if it had been bombed and never rebuilt. I went inside and lay down in a fairly dry corner. And—you'll never believe this—I fell asleep and didn't wake up till seven o'clock. I fell simply awful then and I thought I'd been a fool to run away. But I was more scared than ever to go back, because I thought I'd made a sort of confession of guilt by disappearing. I had hardly any money with me. I thought of going to Sheila, but I didn't want to involve her in it. I got the Tube down to Streatham, where I used to be in digs."

"And there you called on your old friend Bert, and gave

him a story that he believed until he saw the papers next day. Never mind how I know. I've got your movements up to the time you slipped away from there early on Monday morning, and presumably went to this Rosebud place."

"Yes, we'd talked about jobs there and it seemed the only hope. I spent the last of my money on some peroxide and bleached my hair. I had my glasses with me—the ones I use for reading—and started to wear them all the time. I'd seen the paper and knew they were after me, so I had to try to disguise myself. It seemed to work, until you spotted me."

"And how long did you think you could keep up this masquerade? And what about your parents and others who were anxious about you? You really have been very foolish. Still, here you are. And now I'm in the picture, as they say. Now tell me more about this bracelet. I'll tell you what I know first." He related the story as Michael Hexham had told it to him.

"Yes, that's right," Robert said. "A lot of us heard her say it. Do you think that's what the murderer was after, sir?"

"He certainly took it. Now, did you ever have any reason to suppose, apart from that cryptic remark of hers, that she had anything concealed inside that bracelet?"

Robert shook his head. "She never took it off when I was there, and I don't remember any time she wasn't wearing it. I just don't know."

"But you thought, and a lot of other people thought, that it held some kind of clue to the papers she was always boasting about—the papers that held guilty secrets, so to speak?"

"Yes, after that party. It wasn't always there, though. I think she used to move them about from one place to another."

"Why do you think that?"

"Because of something else she said—last term when I was still in with the Communists. She said to me then that she used to collect all sorts of letters and papers and things that might come in useful one day to put pressure on people to do things for the Party. I said it was rather risky to have that stuff lying around, and she said, 'I don't keep it with me, and anybody who wants to find it will have to go half-way to Canterbury.' She knew a lot of people, and perhaps they used to take it in turns to guard the stuff so that nobody could ever be sure what it was."

Ludlow sat silent for a time. Then he got up, walked across to the bookshelves that lined one wall of the room and stood there running his fingers along them as if he was not quite certain what he was looking for. Without taking a book, he suddenly turned and gave a howl of triumph that startled Robert almost out of his chair. As they faced each other, one excited and the other bewildered, neither of them took any notice of the sound of brakes in the street below.

"What a fool I've been," Ludlow said. "Taken in like all the other fools, when the whole thing could have been solved days ago. But I've got less excuse, because it's supposed to be my professional knowledge."

Robert, convinced that his tutor had gone mad, got nervously out of his chair.

"Oh, sit down," said Ludlow. "We can't do anything about it tonight, and it will be quite safe where it is for the moment. If we can bring that evidence along with us when we go to the police tomorrow, it will settle everything. The Inspector will be very surprised, oh yes, very surprised indeed. He's a reasonably well-read man, but he didn't see through this one."

As Robert had not seen through it either and was obviously expected to have done so, he felt distinctly uncomfortable. With the sense of having a rather sticky tutorial, and with his serious situation almost forgotten, he said that perhaps he had better be moving.

"Nonsense," said Ludlow. "You can't go anywhere tonight. By the way, where have you been sleeping? Saturday in an empty house, Sunday on a sofa in Streatham—what about the last two nights?"

"They let me use a sort of attic at the Rosebud."

"You obviously can't go back there. I've got a spare room. Then we can make an early start in the morning, get this silly business settled and resume our normal lives."

"I don't like to give you any more trouble, sir——"

Any further argument about where Robert was to spend the night was cut short by a sharp ring at the doorbell. Ludlow went to open the door. Montero pushed past him into the room, with Springer close behind him. Two large men were at the top of the stairs leading down to the street. Ignoring Ludlow, the Inspector walked across to Robert and said:

"Are you Robert Trent?"

"Yes, I am."

"I am a police officer and I must ask you to accompany me to Cannon Row police station for questioning in connection with the murder of Jenny Hexham last Saturday night."

Robert sat speechless and looked as if he was going to

faint. Ludlow walked over and stood between him and Montero.

"Mr. Trent is my guest," he said, "and he is staying with me for the night."

"I'd advise you to keep out of this, Mr. Ludlow."

"It seems to me that I am already in it. Have you a warrant to arrest Mr. Trent? If it comes to that, have you got a warrant to enter these premises which I happen to occupy?"

"No, I haven't, and if you ask me to go, I will do so. But I shall soon be back with all the warrants I need, and I shall see that nobody leaves this building until I've got them. As you say, sir, you are already in it. If you insist on involving yourself further, I'll have no difficulty in finding a charge to bring against you." He turned to Robert, who was sitting up rigidly. "Are you prepared to accompany me now?"

"You'd better go, Robert," said Ludlow. "I'm sorry things have turned out like this. It would have been better if you had gone to them of your own accord, and I hoped that was still going to be possible. Never mind, it won't be for long."

"How can they have known that I was here?" Robert asked. "Did Henry tell them? Or Sheila—no that's impossible."

"If it's any comfort to you," Montero said patiently, "we were tipped off by Dirty Charlie that you were at the Rosebud. We arrived there just too late to pull you out, but we found that you had just left in the company of a man who answered to the description of Mr. Ludlow. It was obvious from the description the manager gave us that you'd dyed your hair. If people insist on thinking that all policemen are fools, they've only got themselves to blame when they learn differently. Now, are you coming along?"

"One moment," Ludlow said. "You seem to be crediting me with the worst motives for everything I have done so far. But you haven't yet been able to deprive me of my civic rights, and I want to lay a charge of assault against Hugh Quantrough and an unknown man."

Montero grinned. "Yes, I heard there'd been a spot of bother," he said. "We'll be talking to Quantrough in good time. If you've got an urgent case, you'd better take it to your local police station. Unless perhaps you want to charge him with murder?"

"That won't be necessary," said Ludlow. "You shall have your murderer tomorrow. Don't worry, Robert."

Robert did not say anything, as Montero guided him firmly towards the door.

"Please tell me one thing, Inspector," said Ludlow as they were going out. "Where are Jenny Hexham's books?"

Montero stared at him. "Her cousin Michael's got them," he said. "He's been allowed to remove any of her possessions that we're not likely to need in evidence. They were only the usual textbooks that you'd expect a student of her subject to have. But you'd better not do any more interfering with witnesses. And you'd better be somewhere we can find you easily for the next few days. Good night."

They were gone. If Robert could have looked back and seen Ludlow as the door closed, he would have been surprised and shocked to see that his tutor was chuckling happily.

CHAPTER XIII

The students at Mudge Hall, in common with students at other establishments, were more notable for their energy late at night than in the morning. Those of them who were conscious of events at half past eight on the morning after Robert's departure for Cannon Row were astonished to see a tall, thin man tumble out of an ancient car and leap with unusual vigour up the steps in front of the Hall. Many of them recognised him as a don in the English Department and wondered what unfortunate youth had so far dropped behind in his work as to be pursued to his very source at such an intemperate hour. Ludlow, however, was not looking for one of his own erring flock. He strode into the dining-room, under the shocked gaze of the porter who had just taken over from Ferris, and surveyed the sleepy eaters of porridge. His eye falling at last on Steve, he went over to him, uttered the simple words "Come with me", and went out with the air of a man who expects to be obeyed. Steve followed wonderingly until they reached the entrance hall where Ludlow turned on him.

"Why," he demanded, pinning the unfortunate student against the letter-rack, "did you falsely tell Inspector Montero that you did not know Hugh Quantrough?"

"You have asked me this before," said Steve, swallowing the rest of his breakfast. "Why should I not buy books where I wish?"

"I'm not talking about books now. Listen, Robert Trent

is with the police. There may be danger for him, and for all who have shown any connection with this murder. The only hope is to tell the truth; what do you know about Hugh Quantrough?"

Steve looked very frightened. He drew himself up with dignity, threw back his head and looked at once appealing and defiant.

"This Quantrough is a bad man," he said. "He is a Communist and he tries to trap people into joining them. I did not tell the Inspector this because I was afraid that if they found out I am knowing any Communists they would send me away. I am happy here, then she comes, that girl Jenny, and makes me afraid. She wanted me to meet this Quantrough. I went to his shop and bought a book there so that I could look at him."

"Is that the only time you ever saw him?"

"No, it is not. I went one or two times to meetings, with her and with Robert. I was afraid if I did not make some pretence, they would find ways to harm me. Also I was afraid of your police finding out. It has been so awful, and now I am glad she is dead. I know what you are thinking, but I did not kill her."

Now for it, Ludlow thought; this is where I take a big chance.

"Why did you go and tell Quantrough all about me?" he asked.

"You know that too? Yes, you are clever. I went there on Monday, in the morning, because I wanted to see his face as I had triumph over him. You cannot understand that—you are English and you would only lift the eyebrow at such a thing. But I am passionate and I when I hate a person I do not pretend to love. I told him that she was dead and could do no more harm. I told him that you, a very clever man, were—what will I say—yes, investigating this thing and that you would find the truth. Then many secret things would be known, and he would not like it. All this I told him, because I thought you were a friend. Now you tell the police, and you think I have killed her."

Ludlow felt very tired. When would this young man forget the atmosphere of suspicion that had surrounded him since he was a child, and stop dividing everyone he knew into black and white?

"All right, Steve," he said. "I know you didn't kill her, and you have nothing to fear. Please tell me one more thing. You say that on Saturday you gave the keys back to Ferris himself, and I believe that too. But how did you know who it was? Apart from the fact he was there, and wearing the porter's cap, was there anything that made you sure that it was Ferris?"

"Who else should it be?"

"That's what I want to find out. You didn't see his face, did you?"

"No, but I was sure it was Ferris. I saw his hand when he reached to take the keys—his hand with fingers all stained dirty brown from the cigarettes. He is always smoking, it makes me sick."

"Right, Steve. Go and finish your breakfast and stop worrying."

Leaving Steve very puzzled in the hall, Ludlow almost ran upstairs to the top floor, and knocked on Michael Hexham's door. No answer. He tried the door, found it locked, and crossed the corridor to Latham's set of rooms. Latham had just finished breakfast and was having his first cigarette of the day. He looked at Ludlow with distaste, and the look was returned.

"You smoke too much," Ludlow said. "Your fingers are in a disgusting state."

"Is that any business of yours?"

"Perhaps not. Where is Michael Hexham?"

"How should I know? He's probably having breakfast."

"No, I've been in the dining-room, and he's not there. He's not in his own room, either."

"Then he's probably in the common-room reading the papers, or in one of the study-rooms. Now I come to think of it, he is a fairly early riser. The porter will find him for you if you want him."

"I haven't got any time to waste," said Ludlow, "and what I'm going to do is probably better done in his absence. Come on, and bring your set of keys."

"What are you going to do?"

"I'm going to search his room. You've got keys to all the rooms in this block, haven't you? I want you to open his room for me."

"I can't do that. This is outrageous."

Ludlow bent down and put his face very close to Latham's. His manner had changed and he looked like a man who would threaten and carry out his threats. Latham got out of his chair and back across the room, wondering whether his colleague had gone mad.

"Listen to me," said Ludlow. "You weren't so squeamish about walking into my flat when I was out. Inspector Montero will be very interested to hear about that. Also that you had been carrying on an affair with Jenny Hexham and that she was threatening you. And those keys have possibly been used already to enter a student's room—to get into Robert Trent's room last Saturday."

"That's different. I went in then because I thought a rule was being broken."

"I don't mean when you went in with Ferris. I mean when you let yourself in earlier, to wait for Jenny Hexham whom you had decided to kill."

Latham looked terrified. His hand closed on a heavy ornament.

"I shouldn't do anything violent if I were you," Ludlow said with more confidence than he felt. "I can look after myself—I knocked out two men outside a dance-hall last night. And if I'm not inside Michael Hexham's room within five minutes, I'm going to be on the phone to Scotland Yard."

"This is blackmail."

"Call it what you like. This business has got too serious now for the usual polite inanities of well-bred university life. I mean what I say, so get your keys and come."

Trembling with rage or with fear, Latham got the keys from his desk and followed Ludlow into the corridor. Furtively looking to see that no students were in sight, he opened the door of Hexham's room. Ludlow pushed past him and entered the room.

"I can't leave you alone here," Latham said with a pathetic attempt to regain his dignity. "I have a responsibility."

"You can exercise your responsibility in any way that amuses you."

Watched by the outraged Latham, Ludlow moved about the room peering at things. The bookcase first attracted his attention, only to be rejected after a quick glance. A number of books were piled up on the floor under the window. He swooped down on them and discovered to his joy that they were mostly English texts and criticisms. On his hands and knees he started to burrow through them, muttering to himself as he did so.

"She wasn't an exceptional student—sure not to have separate texts of any of the plays except the specially prescribed ones, and *Cymbeline* isn't one of them. Ah, here we are—collected works."

He got to his feet holding a thick volume of Shakespeare and attacked the pages fiercely. In a moment he gave a triumphant shout and held the open book under Latham's nose. It was opened at the last page of *Cymbeline*. Fastened to the page with a small pin was a blue ticket, a receipt for deposit at a railway cloakroom.

"There you are," he shouted, "just as I thought. That's what she meant, not her own bracelet at all. Wouldn't have thought she'd have had so much wit. Poor girl, it killed her, though."

"What are you talking about?" asked Latham.

"Read the play and find out. No time for explanations now. This will give us the last bit of evidence—Jenny Hexham's papers."

Latham recovered himself at these sinister words.

"Do you mean she'd left them in a railway cloakroom?"

"Exactly. Moved them about periodically from one to another. It's a very sensible idea. This one's Victoria, as I thought. We owe that to Sheila Broome."

Latham snatched at the ticket.

"Oh no," said Ludlow, evading him. "Those papers are going to the police. This is no time for private worries. If you didn't kill Jenny Hexham, you haven't got anything serious to worry about."

He neatly removed the ticket and put it in his wallet.

Latham looked as if he was about to attack, when a voice from the doorway made them both turn round.

"May I ask what you are doing in my room?"

It was Michael Hexham, looking as if he was glad of a chance to make himself unpleasant. Latham almost cringed but Ludlow tried to seem unperturbed.

"There is no time for long explanations now," he said. "I hope that by the end of this day a lot of things will be straightened out. For the moment, you must let it go at that."

Michael came farther into the room and shut the door behind him.

"I'm not prepared to let it go at that," he said. "Ever since Jenny was killed there have been attempts to throw suspicion on me. You did your best to convince the police that I had done it, and they were going up and down from my window for hours trying to prove some ridiculous theory. Now I find you in my room and I want an explanation. Perhaps you were here to plant some false evidence."

"Don't be a foolish boy," said Ludlow impatiently. "I'm here not to plant evidence but to find it—evidence that will finish this case as it should be finished. I know now where your cousin hid her papers."

"Well you know more than I do then. I wish she'd never been given that bracelet and that we'd never heard what she said about it."

"What exactly did she say?"

"We've been into all this before—how many more times do you want it? She said, 'You might find it by getting back the bracelet that cast so much doubt on a certain person's character.' That was clear enough, wasn't it?"

"And you thought she had concealed something inside the bracelet that her grandmother had given her?"

"It was obvious. There'd been a lot of fuss and unpleasantness about that bracelet. She didn't mind people knowing about family troubles."

"What would you have thought if she said at another time that the secret was half-way to Canterbury?"

"Did she say that? We don't know anybody down there. She may have had some Communist friends there, I don't know."

Ludlow went to the window and picked up another book from the floor.

"Do you see this?" he asked, pushing it under Michael's nose.

"*Chaucer's Works*. What's that got to do with it. Oh, he wrote the *Canterbury Tales*, didn't he? But I don't see. I mean where's the connection?"

"I cannot waste time on a long explanation," said Ludlow looking at his watch. "I suppose, however, that you are entitled to know something, since she was your cousin and this is your room. The fact is that Jenny never made use of that gold bracelet to conceal anything, and she may or may not have intended to deceive people into thinking that she did. We shall never know now. In fact she adopted the intelligent procedure of leaving her papers, for a week or so at a time, in the cloakroom of a railway station. Somewhere where they would be safe, could be collected at any time without attracting any attention, yet were not actually in her possession. As an extra precaution, she didn't even carry the ticket about with her. She used to hide it in one of her working books. A good plan: a desperate man might search drawers, clothes, a desk—but he would never think of turning the pages of every book in the room. Some time last term she stuck it in her volume of Chaucer, presumably about half-way through the *Canterbury Tales*. The last hiding-place was at the end of *Cymbeline* in her collected Shakespeare."

"But what has the bracelet got to do with all this?" asked Latham.

"Have you ever read *Cymbeline*—or seen it?"

"No, I don't think I have."

"It's not one of the better plays—full of improbabilities and seldom produced. The Old Vic did it a few years ago. It has some of the loveliest poetry, fit to stand with anything he wrote. But he was never happy with the new kind of tragi-comedy——"

"But the bracelet?"

"What? Ah yes, the bracelet. I haven't time to give you a résumé of the very complicated plot. Briefly, Iachimo steals a bracelet from Imogen and uses it to convince her husband Posthumus that he has successfully seduced her. At the end, Iachimo admits his guilt and returns the bracelet:

'And here the bracelet of the truest princess
    That ever swore her faith.'

It's an interesting idea, hiding things in books and making up clues. It would be rather an intelligent sort of treasure-hunt."

The others looked at him with mingled awe and exasperation. Michael was the first to speak.

"So that's what she meant by the bracelet that had cast doubt on somebody's character?"

"Exactly. It was stupid of me not to see it before. I really am quite useless."

No comment was made on this remark. Then Latham moved uneasily.

"What are you going to do with that ticket?" he asked.

"It's going to Inspector Montero."

"Is that necessary?" Michael said.

"Unfortunately, yes. We know that your cousin had papers which certain people very much wanted to get their hands on. There's no doubt that this ticket will lead to those papers. When we've got them, the motive for her death will be established, and perhaps a great deal more."

"Can't all this be forgotten?" said Latham. "You won't do any good by raking up a lot—well—a lot of old scandals. The police will deal with this in their own way."

"I wish these things could be forgotten," Ludlow said. "The police need more proof than they've got before they can charge the murderer. Also, there's been enough underhand work over this business and it's time a few things were brought out into the open."

'Also,' he thought, 'I've stuck my neck out quite far enough without going and destroying material evidence. What hypocrites we all become when we get mixed up in this sort of thing.' Michael Hexham moved towards him, his face white, his hands clenched at his sides.

"If you take that ticket away from here," he said in a low voice, "I'll have a charge of theft brought against you."

"Really, Hexham, don't you want your cousin's murder to be solved?"

"I want things to be left alone. We all know that Robert Trent killed her and that you've been trying to save him by accusing me. You talk about the need to prove motive. Everybody knows what his motive was—he was afraid of her because she had a hold on him. That was probably true of a lot of other people too. Jenny's dead and it's no good for me to pretend I care very much. But I don't want all her misdeeds dragged out and made public. Whatever those papers may show about other people, they won't show much credit for her. Hasn't our family been through enough?"

Ludlow looked at him in an appraising manner. "I'm not sure whether you have exceptional family loyalty or whether you are merely very selfish," he said. "And as for motives, what about the inheritance of a large sum of money? No, I don't think you can stop me taking this little piece of paper away, especially as it's not your property."

"It's certainly not *your* property. And what about breaking into my room while I was out?"

"I break into your room? My dear boy, I did nothing of the kind. Mr. Latham kindly let me in with a special key."

Michael turned accusingly to Latham, who clutched at the doorpost and made gibbering noises.

"Anyway," Ludlow said calmly, "I'm working in close association with Inspector Montero on this case, and it's important that I should get in touch with him as soon as possible. If you like to read *Cymbeline* carefully, you'll understand all about the bracelet and the trouble it caused. Here you are."

He thrust the volume of Shakespeare into Michael's hands and walked out of the room. Latham had been beside himself with mingled fear and rage for several minutes, and with this last gesture his rage triumphed. He ran after Ludlow, shouting threats and demanding that he should be stopped. The students at Mudge Hall were astonished to see one of their well-known lecturers running down the stairs with another in hot pursuit. Ludlow's long stride gave him the advantage, and he was across the entrance hall and down the front steps before Latham had reached the ground floor. For once, Cleopatra responded nobly to the starter, and he was away down the drive while Latham, surrounded by an admiring crowd, shrieked for vengeance in the porch.

As he drove away and headed southwards for the centre of London, Ludlow was surprised to find that he was thoroughly enjoying himself. 'I really ought to take up this sort of thing,' he thought. 'I seem to do rather well in the face of difficulties. It's much more exciting than lecturing. Still, I expect one would get tired of it after a time, and one does certainly get led into some very strange places.'

His next move was clearly to see Montero and give him the ticket. Then a new thought struck him. Why not go to Victoria and get the papers himself? That would be a triumph—to walk up to Montero and present him with what they had all been seeking. 'But I only hope,' he thought, 'that my ideas are right. I've put myself in an awful lot of trouble if they're not.' He turned in the direction of Victoria and joined the stream of traffic that was pouring into London for the new day. From his pleasant role of detective, he began to feel the less pleasant one of criminal. What he had just done was arbitrary, to say the least. Latham was unlikely to do anything to precipitate events, but suppose Michael Hexham got in touch with the police and accused him of illegal entry and removing some of the dead girl's property. He had visions of himself not bursting in on Montero triumphantly but being led before him virtually in chains. He had removed an important piece of evidence, and he had been warned.

After a time, however, his cheerfulness reasserted itself and he tried to concentrate on the task of getting to Victoria. Nevertheless, he still felt a sinking feeling every time the traffic was held up by a policeman, and the sight of a police station nearly made him swerve on the pavement. He felt a new sympathy with what Robert must have been suffering in the past few days. He turned his mind to all those who had become so suddenly and strangely involved in violent death and its consequences. As he crawled on in the thickening traffic, their faces rose one by one in front of him. They came like illustrations to a novel, personalities caught at one moment and held suspended in that act. There was Latham, pressed back against the wall of Ludlow's flat, his stained fingers twisting as he tried to justify his presence there. Steve, waiting for him at the college, his dark eyes intense as he warned against the perils of going any farther. Michael Hexham, only a few minutes ago, arrogantly demanding by what right these things were done. The fat, round face of Henry Prentice, looming over him as he lay on his back in the alley by the dance-hall. Ferris cowering in Springer's grasp while the golden bracelet on the table accused him. And Robert, pale as his white waiter's coat, going away with Montero. For all of them life had changed; for one at least, the worst was soon to come.

He reached Victoria, recklessly parked in front of the station and almost ran towards his goal. Although the journey had seemed endless, it was still scarcely half past nine and the influx of passengers was only just past its peak. He found himself going against a stream of people, all hurrying as if there was not a minute to be lost, terrified of being late. Each one of them had an identity, a special set of loves and hates, of anxieties and desires, but he could see them only as a faceless crowd. His business seemed as overwhelmingly important to him as their various plans undoubtedly did to them. He bore to the right, struggling all the time against the crowd, and at last reached the left-luggage office. It gave the general impression of being shut, since corrugated green shutters had been pulled down for about two-thirds of its length. In a small opening there was a sign, "Withdrawals". Ludlow took his place at the end of a short queue. It seemed that the cloakroom must have been constructed on the lines of a maze, for it took a long time for each article to be produced. At last he was able to hand over the blue ticket. After another wait, during which he feared at any moment to feel a hand on his shoulder, the attendant came back with a shabby brown brief-case, the sort that could be bought by the dozen second-hand. Ludlow took it and turned away. It was as simple as that.

As simple and as foolish. When he stood there actually holding the bag for which a man had been prepared to kill, the station seemed to revolve around him and there was a moment of complete silence, shutting out all the noises and trains and people. What a fool he had been to expose himself to further suspicion and possibly attack for the sake of a gesture. All that was needed to reveal the murderer was in his head. Why on earth had he not told Montero everything on the previous night and spared a great deal of trouble. As he walked towards the exit, he knew that he would have acted in exactly the same way if things had happened over again. This was the love of power. The psychologists would no doubt explain it as compensation for his comparative failure in his profession and in his private life. He wondered whether they included a *deus ex machina* complex among their cases. That certainly seemed to be what he was suffering from. He had an impulse to throw the case away, to run to the bridge and drop it into the river. In a wave of self-pity, he wished he had never got his hands on so much of others' misery. But since he had elected to play the part of Fortune, he could do nothing but go on.

He came out into the open, where buses fumed and slid to and from their moorings, and the anonymous crowd still streamed in all directions. He went over to the battered form of Cleopatra and shifted the brief-case to his left hand as he took hold of the door. The very sky seemed to be blotted out as an enormous policeman, even taller than himself and much broader, put a restraining hand on his outstretched arm.

CHAPTER XIV

Inspector Montero looked down from a high window on the Thames glittering in the low-slanting sun. A river tug glided its train of barges downstream. A police patrol-launch foamed its way towards Westminster Bridge and was envied by the observer far above. Montero did not rate one of the largest or most comfortable offices in Scotland Yard but at least he had a good view of the river. Springer, impassive as ever, sat at the smaller of the two desks in the room and waited for his superior to speak, Montero turned from the window, threw himself down in his chair, and stabbed the blotter viciously with a paper-knife.

"We're scrambling, Jack," he said. "That boy hasn't put us any farther forward. If he's holding out, he's a damned good liar and a tougher character than he looks."

"We can't hold him much longer, sir, can we?" said Springer.

"No, we've got to charge him or turn him loose pretty soon. There isn't enough to hang it on him yet, unless we can find a flaw in his story. Which I can't. But if he didn't do it, who did?"

"If we let him go and have him watched, he may lead us on to something."

"Could do. But we're going to look precious fools, after putting out a call for him all this time, if we have to release him as soon as we get our hands on him.

Whether he actually did it or not, he's not the only one who knows more than he's told us so far. Let's get it down on paper and look at it again."

He picked up a pad and wrote a name at the top.

"First, what's Quantrough doing in all this? He's made it quite clear that he's got some interest in the case—but what? He seems to be after Ludlow rather than Trent—he's had him watched, probably broken into his flat, and certainly attacked him. I don't think Dirty Charlie knows any more than he's told us; he always squeals when we get hold of him. So we've still got to find out what Quantrough is really up to. All right. Now, what about Ludlow?"

"Ah, what about him, you may well say," Springer said.

"Yes, I have. Is he covering up Trent because he knows he's innocent or because he knows he's guilty? A man of his intelligence isn't going to all this trouble on trust and probability. If he sails much nearer the wind I'll pull him in—but there's nothing we can do so far. I only hope that he's basically on our side, because I don't fancy him as an opponent. If only we could find those blasted papers, we might know whether he's got any more interest in this case than he pretends to have."

"You still think she was blackmailing him, sir?"

"It's more than likely, but likelihood isn't enough. So Ludlow's still a query as well. And the third thing is—you tell me."

"Keys."

"Yes, every time we come back to those keys. They may not be of any importance—there's not all that difficulty about getting into the room. But who is lying about them, and why?"

Springer coughed hesitantly, and looked at Montero like a hopeful retriever.

"I've been thinking about that," he said. "Suppose this Pole, Steve, was in a plot with Trent—because they were both being threatened by the girl for not wanting to be Communists. He got the keys, for a proper purpose that he could explain away, and slipped the important one to Trent. Then he left them on the desk, and swore blind that he'd given them back to Ferris, who ought to have checked them anyway. Trent gave his own key to the girl, and made sure that her cousin knew about it, so that it would look as if he couldn't get back into his room before her. He made Prentice think he was going out, then fooled everybody by slipping back into the room and waiting for her. Ludlow's being threatened or blackmailed as well, and tries to throw false clues all over the place. How's that, sir? It's just a little thing of my own."

Montero thought for a few moments, meanwhile drawing on his pad a face that looked remarkably like Ludlow.

"It's neat," he said, "perhaps too neat. It explains quite a lot. Somehow, I don't see Steve standing aside if there was any killing to be done. If it was Trent who had got the keys and Steve who'd run away—I suppose the next thing is to get hold of Quantrough. We've got enough to bring him in, and he's obviously lined up with the Communists in some way. Which may be important. Because, if she was on the verge of leaving the Party, we ought to be looking not among her opponents but among her old associates."

"Remember that we've only got Trent's word for the fact she was leaving—and Ludlow's."

"And Mrs. Reddle's. None of them ideal witnesses from our point of view."

"Do you think Trent may have been pretending about not being interested any more—a bluff he was put up to by the Commies themselves?"

"To be honest, I don't know what I think at the moment."

The telephone rang. Montero picked it up with a growl, prepared to turn to a more appropriate noise if it was the Assistant Commissioner. It was in fact the desk-sergeant below.

"Yes? I can't see anybody now, I'm working on a case —says he's got evidence about the Hexham murder? —what's his name?—Ludlow—send him up to me right away—and see that he gets here, because he's a pretty slippery customer."

When Ludlow was ushered into Montero's office a few minutes later, he did not look at all slippery, merely a little more dishevelled than usual. He carried a shabby brief-case which he placed carefully on the desk.

"I think you've been looking for this," he said.

"What is it?" asked Montero.

"The bag containing the papers that Jenny Hexham was using to bring pressure on a number of people."

"But where did you get it?"

"From the left-luggage cloakroom at Victoria. The ticket was hidden in one of her books. I don't blame you for not having found it—a certain specialist knowledge was needed. By the way, I wish you would tell your policemen not to usurp the teaching function."

"What on earth do you mean?"

"I left my car at Victoria while I went to get the bag. I was away only a few minutes and there was a great open space in front of the station with plenty of room all round me. When I came back—and after doing work on your behalf too—a policeman was standing by the car. He said that I would be summoned for obstruction —obstruction by a small car in an area like that! Not content with this, he pompously gave me a lecture about other people catching trains in a hurry, and taxis and buses and the flow of traffic. He said I ought to show consideration for others. I haven't come to my age to be taught ethics by——"

"That's nothing to do with me," said Montero. "That will be Traffic or perhaps he was Railways. If you want to make a complaint—but never mind about that. What exactly is in this bag?"

"You'd better open it and find out. It's locked—not that I would interfere in things that don't concern me," he added virtuously.

"Do you realise that the contents of this bag may help to convict Robert Trent?"

"No, because he didn't do it. I hope you won't keep him much longer, or he'll be falling behind on his work. Well, well, I must get along."

"You can't go now," Montero said.

Ludlow drew himself up and gave the Inspector a withering look.

"I do not think that you have power to detain me for a parking offence," he said, "and so far as I am aware I have committed no other crime. Anyway, you just said that you were not concerned with traffic. I have work to do, and I have already lost a great deal of time over this affair. If you have any more to say to me, you will find me in college."

He stalked out of the room. Montero put his hand

on the telephone. Then he sighed like a man who knows that he has met his match and picked up the brief-case.

"Send for somebody who can open this thing without damaging it," he said.

Ludlow got away from Scotland Yard without any more lectures from the police and drove northwards again. The early traffic had thinned out and he went as fast as Cleopatra could carry him. He was in the college soon after ten. The first lectures had started and only a few belated students scuttled across the courtyard in front of the main building. The porter on duty was surprised to see Ludlow turn in the opposite direction from his usual walk to the rooms of the English Department. He moved slowly but with determination. What had to be done now was the last step in a succession of weary days that already seemed like months. The excitement of the hunt had died in him and he felt no enthusiasm for the last part of his task. He almost wished that he had left things alone, trusting the police to find the solution for themselves. He went towards the huge block that housed all the Faculty of Science, a yellow monstrosity about which he had often been scathing to his unfortunate colleagues who worked there. This morning he scarcely noticed his surroundings. Without any of his usual remarks about the neglect of the Arts, he started to climb the stairs that led to the chemistry laboratories.

It was a long time since he had set foot in a place like this. The acrid smell, the rows of bottles, the overalled figures at the benches, all reminded him of some of the less enjoyable parts of his schooldays. A young lecturer, whom he knew slightly, was in charge of the proceedings and was lounging in a bored way at the far end of the room. Ludlow approached him.

"Forgive my entering this forbidden territory of esoteric rites," he said, "but I want to talk to Henry Prentice. There is something which it is essential that I should ask him."

"Prentice? He's in one of the smaller labs—through there. He's working on his own research."

"Thank you. I fear that I shall have to divert him from gazing into test-tubes for a few minutes."

Prentice, however, was not gazing into test-tubes. He was sitting on a high stool entering results in a note-book. He got up, with a look of surprise, when he saw Ludlow.

"Ah, Mr. Prentice, I am sorry to interrupt these matters to which so much importance is attached today, but I need your help. I missed you when I called at Mudge Hall this morning."

"Yes," said Prentice with a grin, "I heard that you left rather quickly."

"Quite so, and I've been busy since then. Now you're a scientist, and you can tell me something I want to know. What happens when one of the fuses at the Hall is blown out—I mean, how many rooms does it affect?"

"Well, that's not really my line, sir," said Prentice. "I'm a chemist, not a physicist, but I can answer that one easily enough. The floors are wired to separate fuse-boxes."

"You mean that if a student in one room, by intent or accident, caused a fuse to go, all the other rooms on his floor would be affected—lights and wall-points and every-thing?"

"That's right."

"Thank you. I thought it was probably like that and it's a help to have it confirmed. Now tell me something else. Did you know that the police came for Robert Trent at my flat last night, after we had dropped you?"

"They came for Robert? No, I'd no idea. I say, sir, I hope you don't think that I——"

"No, I know that you didn't tell them where he was, and I know who did. We may be convinced that Robert is innocent, but it's going to be much more difficult to convince the police. Inspector Montero seems to be quite sure that everything is solved. In short, there's no use denying that Robert is in some danger. I think I can save him, but I'm going to need your help. You can have him freed within an hour if you wish. Will you help me?"

"But of course, I'll do anything I can. Robert and I are quite good friends, and in any case I'd want to help a chap in trouble. But I don't see exactly what I can do."

Ludlow picked up the pencil with which Prentice had been jotting down results. He tapped it against his teeth and looked hard at the chemical balance which hung motionless in its glass case on the bench. When he next spoke it was with the judicial air of an oral examiner summing up the chances of a candidate.

"Mr. Prentice," he said, "you have the reputation of being a very able young man. I know nothing of what goes on within these four chemical walls, but I am assured that you are likely to make some mark in your field of study. You also have the reputation of being industrious and ambitious. Am I far wrong?"

Prentice blushed. "I'm certainly keen to get on," he said.

"Quite so. And you have got a very good first degree and are now making progress with your research. It i unfortunate for you that you have got yourself into a position where neither ability nor ambition is of any account."

"Just what do you mean by that, Mr. Ludlow?"

"I mean that the bag containing all the documents which Jenny Hexham was anxious to conceal is now in the possession of Inspector Montero at Scotland Yard."

Prentice looked surprised but unmoved. "So they've found it?" he said.

"It has been found. A lot of people would have liked to get their hands on it first, including one man who had already committed murder in his anxiety to have it."

"That's all very interesting. But why have you come to tell me this?"

"Because, Mr. Prentice, you feared the revelation of certain things that Jenny Hexham knew. You feared it so much that you killed her."

Prentice looked at him with wide-open eyes. Then he threw back his head and laughed as if he had just heard the best joke of his life. He leaned on the bench convulsed with laughter, until he had to take off his glasses and wipe them. At last, pushing back his disordered hair, he was able to splutter a few words.

"Really, Mr. Ludlow, with all respect I must say that you are making a fool of yourself. I scarcely knew Jenny Hexham and I'm not a bit interested in any papers she may have had. If this is an attempt on your part to save Robert Trent, I'm afraid it's going to fail. You'd better look for an easier scapegoat."

"Very well. Let us look back for a moment to last Saturday, the night when the murder was committed. You have said that you did not leave your room after Robert left you about ten o'clock, until you heard the excitement when the murder was discovered."

"I've been through all that before. I told you and I told the police, and you won't get me to alter the statement because it happens to be true."

"For the greater part of that time, you were listening to a symphony on your record-player? And you did not interrupt that recording even for a moment?"

"I've already said so. What's the point of all this?"

"Simply that you could not have heard it without interruption. During that period the students in a room on the same floor caused the lights to fuse. You told me a few minutes ago that a fuse affects the whole floor, including the wall-points—into one of which your record-player was plugged. I had an opportunity of observing that when I spoke to you that evening. You were unaware of the break, because you were not in your room at the time."

Prentice was no longer laughing. He swallowed heavily and forced himself to smile.

"Really, this all rather silly. Yes, there was a fuse but I didn't think it worth mentioning. I was asked only if I was in my room, which I was."

"You said categorically that you listened to Beethoven's Fifth Symphony without a break or interruption. If you wish to amend your first statement, it is your duty to call on Inspector Montero in order to do so."

"I don't think it's all that important."

"He may think differently. At what time did the fuse go?"

"I—I don't remember."

"No, you don't remember because when it happened you were not in your room. You were not on that floor. You were in Robert Trent's room on the floor above, waiting for Jenny Hexham to come back there so that you could strangle her and take the bracelet which you thought contained the clue that you wanted."

"I admit nothing. Do you think any case can be built up on a little thing like this?"

"Not on this alone. Remember that the documents which gave her a hold over you are being examined at Scotland Yard. Now will you go forward and confess?"

"No!" Prentice almost screamed the word at him. "All right, perhaps I did have a bit of trouble with her. But so did plenty of other people. A lot of men would have liked to kill her, for different reasons. I don't happen to be the one who did it."

"You happen to be just that. Because you had a stronger motive than the others—the fear of exposure for Communist activities. I have already remarked that you have the name of being both able and ambitious. I will add a third epithet—you are ruthless when anything seems likely to stand in the way of your ambition. You knew that you had done enough to jeopardise your career as a scientist and you wanted to make sure that it would never be known. I'm afraid that your promising career is over before it has begun. I'm giving you the chance to save something from the wreck. If you give yourself up before they come to get you, it may make things a little easier."

Prentice's eyes were like dull steel. He backed towards the long window that gave light to the small laboratory.

"No," Ludlow shouted, "don't do that. Whatever you've done so far, that's the worst way out."

"Did you think I was going to jump out?" Prentice sneered. "You won't get rid of me so easily as that, I can assure you."

"I was mistaken then. I thought you might have forgotten that there was no fire-escape from that window. You can't get away from this room as you did from Robert's last Saturday—and your room is not directly below for you to lower yourself in and pretend nothing had happened."

The mask dropped at last. "Damn you," said Prentice very quietly. "Damn you for interfering in things that ought to have been left alone."

"Those fire-escapes are remarkable things," Ludlow went on as if the other had not spoken. "A big man like you goes down as slowly and comfortably as a small chap like Robert Trent. If the night had been dry, there'd have been nothing to suggest that anyone but Robert had gone that way."

"What do you mean?"

"Never mind. Now will you come with me?"

"No. If you think you can make an accusation against me and get it to stick, then go ahead; I'm not going to make it any easier for you."

"Surprising as it may seem, it is for you that I want to make things easier. If you give yourself up, you will save a lot of trouble for yourself. I'm no lawyer, but I have followed a number of trials for murder. This is the sort of case where your best defence will be to admit the facts and plead that there was no intention to kill. If you think I'm doing this to have you punished, you're wrong. If nobody else was in danger—but that's a dark path and I'll lose my way if I try to follow it. Come along."

Prentice said nothing. He very carefully closed the note-book on the bench and laid the pencil beside it. He took off his white coat and hung it in a cupboard from which he took his own sports jacket. He nodded to Ludlow and opened the door for him to go out. Twenty surprised pairs of eyes watched them as they walked through the main laboratory. The young lecturer in charge looked as if he was going to say something to them, but there was a sign in both their faces that forbade speech. Even the few students who had not heard that Ludlow was interested in the murder, knew that these men were walking where they could not and must not follow. The stairs down to the ground floor had never been so long or echoed so strangely. The low autumn sunlight had never struck such strange black shadows as when they walked across the courtyard to where Cleopatra was parked among the students' bicycles. They got in and Ludlow backed out, swung in an arc and drove through the gates. It was less than ten minutes since he had entered the building.

After they had left the college, they drove in silence for some time. They had turned out into the main road when Prentice gave an exclamation. It was the first sound he had uttered since his surrender.

"What's the matter?" Ludlow asked him.

"Please stop. There's something I want to tell you."

Ludlow drew into the side of the road. After the early traffic, it had become almost deserted. The few vehicles that passed them gave the impression of being already late. Prentice twisted in his seat so that he was facing Ludlow.

"Are you really going to give me away?" he asked.

"I'm going to give you the chance of making a full voluntary confession. I'm only glad that you've been sensible enough to agree."

"And if I still refuse, are you going to tell the police what you've told me that you know?"

"I shall have no alternative. But the incriminating evidence of the documents will probably make it unnecessary."

"That won't be enough, and you know it. Even if they suspect that I had the strongest motive for killing her, they can't prove it. If you keep quiet, they'll never know about the fuse and they can't start to break my story. And they're bound to let Robert go soon, because they can't prove anything against him either. For the last time, are you going to forget it all?"

"For the last time, I am not."

Prentice reached out as slowly and casually as if he was taking a beaker from the shelf. His hands were immensely strong. For the second time that week, Ludlow felt the life being choked out of him.

"This is really rather a pity," Prentice said very quietly as his grip tightened on Ludlow's throat, "but you do see, don't you, that you leave me with no alternative? When you are unconscious, I shall set fire to the car. You've noticed that we are on a downward slope here? I shall release the handbrake, and if I get slightly burned in the process it will build up my story that the car suddenly burst into flames and then I jumped clear and was unable to pull you out. By the time you are pulled out by somebody else, there won't be any of my marks left on you."

With his ebbing thoughts, Ludlow tried frantically to get Prentice to understand that his story would never hold, that he would be convicted of double murder—capital murder. He could make no sound. Suddenly the pressure relaxed as unexpectedly as it had begun. The red haze dissolved back into vision. Prentice was outside the car with Montero and Springer holding him firmly by the arms.

"We were coming up after you," Montero said conversationally to Ludlow, "to ask you a few questions. We passed your old crock at the side of the road—Sergeant Springer spotted the number and I turned round to come up behind you. Good job for you I did, it seems. Aren't you getting a bit tired of playing detectives?"

For once Ludlow was unable to answer. His throat felt too painful for him to counter the insults to himself and to the beloved Cleopatra. Prentice turned his head and looked straight at Montero with his big, serious eyes.

"I'm glad I've seen you here," he said. "I was just on my way to call on you. I want to make a statement about the murder of Jenny Hexham."

CHAPTER XV

"I never thought that I would be led to the truth by any kind of electrical device," Ludlow said. "I have resisted and will continue to resist the overweening pride of the scientists and the cult of their diabolical inventions. One must admit, however, that they have their uses."

He was safely back in his room in college the day after the arrest of Henry Prentice. Robert had spent a confused five minutes after his release, trying to thank his benefactor before he was sent away and told to get on with some work to make up for lost time. Now Ludlow sat at his desk and looked benevolently at Montero who, in the students' chair, was for once willing to listen to him. He had come over to give the formal thanks which the excited events of the previous day had made impossible. His worst enemies, when they gathered in dark corners, had to admit that Montero was a fair-minded man and one who gave credit when and where it was due. Basking in a handsome apology and an official expression of gratitude, Ludlow was in one of his good moods.

"It wasn't only the business of the fuse, of course," he went on, "but that was enough to tell me that he was lying. A small lie may conceal a bigger one. You've probably noticed that."

"Yes," said Montero humbly, "I have noticed it."

"The first thing was the fire-escape. When I entered the room, it was obvious at once that somebody had gone out by the window. I crossed to see if there was any sign of him, and it was the free part of the escape that caught my attention—I mean the part that was hanging loose and apparently hadn't been used. You assumed that Trent had gone down that way, and of course you were right. But he wasn't the first: the other part *had* been used. I touched it and found that it was quite wet. Now you'll remember that the wind was blowing the rain against the other side of the building. The webbing sling could not possibly have got so wet just hanging in the shelter of the window; it must have been out in the open. When Robert told me how he had found it hanging, my belief was confirmed."

"But you didn't know at the time how far down the first escaper had gone," Montero pointed out. "It could have been anybody at all."

"Quite so. And that first night I put only a small query against Prentice's name. I naturally began to look for other things that would fit. Early next day a man, heavily disguised, called at Jenny Hexham's lodgings and tried to get at her things. By the way, I found out yesterday that he borrowed that beard from a student in the Hall who had connections with the Dramatic Society. The silly boy never thought to tell us about it, or we might have been saved a lot of trouble. Anyway, Prentice went along disguised. But he forgot to disguise his hands. Mrs. Reddle told you—and me—that her visitor was a heavy smoker. How could she have known that? In the short time he was there, she could not have had any basis for that opinion. What she meant was that his fingers were stained brown. Now it is important to think less of people's opinions than of what causes them to form those opinions. You were looking for a heavy smoker; I was looking for a man with brown fingers. It is not only smokers who get brown stains on their fingers. Those whose work brings them into contact with chemicals, especially acids, often show the same marks. Prentice is a chemist, conducting post-graduate research."

"I didn't fail to notice that his fingers were brown," said Montero, a little huffily. "He just wasn't on our list of suspects. But I won't make excuses, Mr. Ludlow. I did slip up a bit over that one."

"It could happen to anyone," said Ludlow magnanimously, having gained his point. "Even that would probably not have made certain that Prentice was the murderer. But his anxiety about Robert seemed to me to be suspicious."

"Just what I felt about you," Montero said with a laugh.

"But I had reason to feel responsible for his welfare. Sheila Broome, who had known Robert for a long time, knew of no particular friendship with Prentice. When Prentice began to show an interest in her as well, my suspicions went a bit farther. He was hoping that she knew where Robert was hiding and that he could find out from her. You can understand that he realised that Robert represented a threat to him—a threat that he had never expected to exist, because Robert was supposed to have gone out before ten o'clock. As things were, he might have seen Prentice actually going down from the window."

"If he'd found him, we might have had another murder on our hands," Montero said. "He's not the sort to let anything stand in his way."

"I discovered that yesterday, nearly to my cost. As I

was saying, Prentice condemned himself in several ways. The next one was given out by Mrs. Reddle. When I talked to her on Tuesday afternoon, she told me about Jenny being frightened of a student who was a Communist. She was afraid he might poison her. Now notice, Inspector, that she didn't say kill, or murder, or strangle. She said *poison*, and poison is, I think, not often a man's way of killing. But it would be easier for a research chemist, with access to a laboratory, than it would be for most men. I must admit that all the talk of Communists nearly threw me off the trail. There was no reason for thinking that Prentice was a member of that Party, and I came to the conclusion that he was simply because it was the only thing that fitted the facts. For a long time I thought he was in league with Quantrough, but that's something I still haven't been able to work out. I think they were working independently."

"You're right again," said Montero. "I told you that we picked up Dirty Charlie on Wednesday night, as soon as he'd finished with you. One of my men was trailing him, just waiting for him to put a foot wrong. When he'd spoken to you, we slapped a charge of insulting behaviour on him and told him to start talking. He knows us, and we know him—and he talked plenty. Quantrough had employed him to follow you, find out what you were up to and try to scare you off it. Charlie didn't know what it was all about, except that it was worth a few pounds to him. He's already reported to Quantrough your conversation about the Rosebud, so that's why you were attacked there. He may have meant to knock off Robert that night. Anyway, Charlie tipped us off just too late. We must have arrived just after you got away."

"Yes," Ludlow said with a reminiscent smile, "you did. But what was Quantrough after all the time? Where did he come into things?"

"By what we can get from Charlie, it's your own fault for making too strong an impression on him. First, Steve gave you a build-up; then you went yourself and evidently scared him more than you thought. When he first heard of Jenny being killed, his only thought was for certain documents in her possession which he didn't want to fall into the wrong hands—meaning, from his point of view, our Special Branch. When he found a man posted at her lodgings, and you descended on him the same afternoon, he thought there was a threat to him personally. He seemed to have come to the conclusion that you were some sort of counter-agent and that you were after Robert for the sake of her papers which he had managed to get away with. That's why he had you followed and then prepared to act on the information that was picked up for him by Charlie. Also why he broke into your flat, hoping that the papers were there."

"You mean that he wanted Robert not for being the man who killed Jenny Hexham but the one who had thereby got access to her papers."

"Exactly. He was at the Rosebud with a confederate —who we'll get in due course—very likely with the idea of seizing Robert Trent at the end of the evening. You spoiled that game, and he tried to snatch him off you. We'll get him on the assault charge—you'll have to come along and make a statement about that—then we'll hold him while Special Branch goes to work. We'll oppose bail, on the grounds that we are inquiring into more serious charges." Montero looked as if he was about to purr.

"Is he really deeply involved with Communism?" Ludlow asked.

"That remains to be seen. It may be on an international espionage level, or he may be just a small-timer who didn't want his respectable front to be broken, for business reasons. The fact that he knew how to get hold of a regular crook like Dirty Charlie means that he's got a finger in the criminal world one way or another. But somehow his methods haven't got the mark of big stuff on them. Never mind him. Tell me more about Prentice. It's his case that I've got to build up now."

"Well, as I found out more, it seemed less and less likely that Jenny had been threatening Robert. She was getting out of the Party, and an independent witness who saw both of them on the evening she was killed didn't notice any sign of a quarrel between them. Prentice was the only one who said that Robert was agitated. And that, coupled with the other things, suggested that it was Prentice himself who was being threatened. Robert was what you would probably call small-time stuff. He's got mildly involved with the Communists through a holiday visit and a lot of clever propaganda. Prentice was a much bigger fish to hook. Whereas Robert was only a student of English, Prentice was a chemist, a scientist, one of the new élite. The time will come when this country will pay for its neglect of the arts and its sycophantic parrot-cries of science—industry—technology——"

"Yes, yes," said Montero soothingly. "Yes, we know that Prentice had got in with the Communists in his finals year—he's already admitted that. I think it was a sort of intellectual curiosity that first drew him in. But he soon saw that it wouldn't do him any good to be mixed up with them, especially if his line was going to be in governmental research, as he apparently hoped. He tried to break with them, but he'd committed himself too far—even so far as passing on some information about a job of research going on in your labs. here. As far as I can judge, it wasn't of any real importance, but Jenny made a big thing out of it and threatened to use it as documentary evidence against him. She was going to send it to the college authorities anonymously if he didn't do more. In fact, as you guessed, he was being threatened by her in exactly the same way as he said she was threatening Robert. Last Saturday was his golden opportunity. If he'd only known that she was on the verge of leaving the Party—it's ironical when you come to think of it. Hardy would have appreciated that one, Mr. Ludlow."

"Indeed he would. And of course Prentice thought he would get from her bracelet the clue to where the paper was hidden."

"Yes. Now he has just made a statement that he never intended to kill her, only to make her unconscious and steal her bracelet so that he could get back the evidence that she had against him. That's presumably going to be his line of defence and it may be true. He's a powerful fellow and he may just have squeezed too hard. But it won't do him much good. If he set out to commit a felony and in the course of it killed somebody, it comes to murder. And all the time she'd hidden the clue somewhere else!"

"By the way," said Ludlow, "was there much in the bag?"

"It was a pitiful collection of rubbish. A few Communist pamphlets, letters from students who'd got themselves caught up with her Party, a few love-letters.

Your colleague Latham has a pretty hot style when he tries."

"And not long ago you thought it was me," Ludlow said. "I suppose I'm old enough to feel flattered. Does all that have to become public?"

"It's no concern of ours; he can have his letters back quite soon. No, I don't think there was anything in that famous bag that we need have taken a second look at. She was romancing, exaggerating the importance of what she knew, because it gave her a sense of power over other people. She had her little bit of excitement and died for it. And all those who were sweating blood over what she might do to them could have slept easy."

The two men were silent for a moment, both thinking of the crumpled figure on the floor with the scarf round her throat.

"But I'm spoiling your story," Montero said. "What's your reconstruction of the actual murder?"

"If Prentice has made a statement," said Ludlow, almost pouting like a child, "there's no point in my going on."

"Please do, it may be of great assistance to me in checking his story."

"Ah. Well, that Saturday evening, Robert went down to his room—not because he was in trouble but just for a chat with one of the few students who was in the Hall at that time. Prentice saw that his chance had come. He did all he could to encourage Robert to go out, and thought that he'd succeeded. Robert fully intended to go to the dance but it was raining so hard that he stayed in. Prentice knew that Jenny would have to go back for her bag and coat, and get out before half past ten. His only problem was to get into the room and take her by surprise. Then he heard Steve going down and shouting to Pratt that he was going for the keys. That was when Prentice showed the keenness of his brain and the quality of his nerve. He knew that it was nearly time for Ferris to go and see to the boilers. He waited till he heard Steve coming back upstairs, then he ran down and got behind the empty porter's desk. Putting on Ferris's cap and bending behind the desk, he was convincing enough for Steve to put the keys into his outstretched hand without a second thought. Whether he intended it or not, his brown-stained fingers helped to build up the illusion. As soon as Steve had gone, he took the key he wanted and left the others on the desk where Ferris found them later. So you see, neither Steve nor Ferris was deliberately lying."

"Yes, I must admit that one held me up for a long time. I ought to know by now that the simplest solution is usually the right one. But I was right from the start in thinking that the murderer waited for her there in the room."

"Yes, he waited. And probably no one will ever know what thoughts went through his mind there, what fear mingled with ambition, what hatred of her and of his own folly. He may have waited with the resolve to kill, or he may be telling the truth when he said that he didn't intend to go so far. Eventually she came. He heard the quick, light steps that were different from the tread of the men he was accustomed to hear in the Hall. She opened the door with the key Robert had given her leaving it in the lock in the careless way of students, so that he could get back later. Perhaps Prentice never realised that, or perhaps he thought it would be a good thing to have Robert's key found there. He strangled her

Probably he caught her from behind as she was reaching for the light-switch. He pushed a chair under the handle of the door, though he had no real expectation of being interrupted. He had probably already taken the keys from her bag while he was waiting. He wrenched off the bracelet that was to give him the clue—and found nothing there. Then came the interruption that he had not expected. Somebody was turning the key and pushing the door: in a moment the chair would slip away and he would be found. He didn't know then that it was Robert, and he didn't care. His only way out was through the window, and he used it. I don't suppose he had time to use the escape properly—just seized hold of the sling with his hands as Robert did later. Luckily for him, his own room was immediately below. He checked himself with his feet on the window-sill and struggled into his own room. He dropped the bracelet, accidentally or in disgust, and it fell through the grating where Ferris found it next morning. Prentice had time to put on dry clothes, tidy himself and reappear when the noise started upstairs. To reappear as a model student and rebuke me for interfering with evidence."

"He was right there, anyway," said Montero with a grin. "And the rest we know. He went off next day with her keys to Shepherd's Bush but drew another blank. Then there was nothing he could do but wait, while you very neatly drew the net around him."

Ludlow looked highly pleased with himself. Then he fell silent. One life had gone, another was ruined. A pool of slime had been stirred up and was still spreading its ripples wider. And behind the girl who had died in trying to live out a magazine-story there stretched a fabric of plots and counterplots across the world. The curse on this generation was a curse that turned men's minds against each other. A prophet's vision had broken into a nightmare from which there was no waking yet. By her own choice, Jenny Hexham had made herself into a cipher, to be valued or discarded as her belief was shared or rejected. She had lived in a fantasy of importance. She had died a lonely, frightened girl on a wet night at the turning of the year.

Ludlow roused himself and looked accusingly at Montero as if his thoughts were being read. The two men had shared something that was not easily to be forgotten, that could lead to a friendship or to a deep hostility. They both held positions of some respect and authority, but now they sat and looked at each other across a desk, two puzzled and uncertain men alone with a memory. There was a timid knock at the door. Robert Trent came in, and nearly ran out again at the sight of Montero.

"Yes, what is it?" Ludlow asked.

"It's time for my tutorial, sir."

"Goodness me, so it is. I've never forgotten a time before, never in all my life. I'm slipping, I'm getting old and useless. It's the result of keeping bad company."

"I'd better get along," said Montero, smiling.

"Yes, please."

"I'll give you a ring when we want you."

"All right. But remember that I'm a very busy man and I can't run out every time a policeman needs to know something."

As they shook hands, they understood each other well enough. Robert took the seat that Montero had left, and Ludlow faced him across the desk.

"Well, begin reading your essay. It was 'The Precursors of the Romantic Movement', if I remember rightly."

"I'm sorry, sir, I haven't been able to do an essay this week."

Ludlow pressed the tips of his fingers together and looked severe.

"Mr. Trent, I believe you have had a good deal of spare time during the past week. Can you give me any good reason why you have not done an essay for me?"

THE PERENNIAL LIBRARY MYSTERY SERIES

Ted Allbeury

THE OTHER SIDE OF SILENCE P 669, $2.84
"In the best le Carré tradition . . . an ingenious and readable book."
—*New York Times Book Review*

PALOMINO BLONDE P 670, $2.84
"Fast-moving, splendidly technocratic intercontinental espionage tale
. . . you'll love it." —*The Times* (London)

SNOWBALL P 671, $2.84
"A novel of byzantine intrigue. . . ."—*New York Times Book Review*

Delano Ames

CORPSE DIPLOMATIQUE P 637, $2.84
"Sprightly and intelligent."
—*New York Herald Tribune Book Review*

FOR OLD CRIME'S SAKE P 629, $2.84

MURDER, MAESTRO, PLEASE P 630, $2.84
"If there is a more engaging couple in modern fiction than Jane and
Dagobert Brown, we have not met them." —*Scotsman*

SHE SHALL HAVE MURDER P 638, $2.84
"Combines the merit of both the English and American schools in the
new mystery. It's as breezy as the best of the American ones, and has
the sophistication and wit of any top-notch Britisher."
—*New York Herald Tribune Book Review*

E. C. Bentley

TRENT'S LAST CASE P 440, $2.50
"One of the three best detective stories ever written."
—Agatha Christie

TRENT'S OWN CASE P 516, $2.25
"I won't waste time saying that the plot is sound and the detection
satisfying. Trent has not altered a scrap and reappears with all his old
humor and charm." —Dorothy L. Sayers

Andrew Bergman

THE BIG KISS-OFF OF 1944 P 673, $2.84

"It is without doubt the nearest thing to genuine Chandler I've ever come across. . . . Tough, witty—very witty—and a beautiful eye for period detail. . . ." —Jack Higgins

HOLLYWOOD AND LEVINE P 674, $2.84

"Fast-paced private-eye fiction." —San Francisco Chronicle

Gavin Black

A DRAGON FOR CHRISTMAS P 473, $1.95

"Potent excitement!" —New York Herald Tribune

THE EYES AROUND ME P 485, $1.95

"I stayed up until all hours last night reading The Eyes Around Me, which is something I do not do very often, but I was so intrigued by the ingeniousness of Mr. Black's plotting and the witty way in which he spins his mystery. I can only say that I enjoyed the book enormously." —F. van Wyck Mason

YOU WANT TO DIE, JOHNNY? P 472, $1.95

"Gavin Black doesn't just develop a pressure plot in suspense, he adds uninfected wit, character, charm, and sharp knowledge of the Far East to make rereading as keen as the first race-through." —Book Week

Nicholas Blake

THE CORPSE IN THE SNOWMAN P 427, $1.95

"If there is a distinction between the novel and the detective story (which we do not admit), then this book deserves a high place in both categories." —New York Times

END OF CHAPTER P 397, $1.95

". . . admirably solid . . . an adroit formal detective puzzle backed up by firm characterization and a knowing picture of London publishing." —New York Times

HEAD OF A TRAVELER P 398, $2.25

"Another grade A detective story of the right old jigsaw persuasion." —New York Herald Tribune Book Review

MINUTE FOR MURDER P 419, $1.95

"An outstanding mystery novel. Mr. Blake's writing is a delight in itself." —New York Times

THE MORNING AFTER DEATH P 520, $1.95

"One of Blake's best." —Rex Warner

A PENKNIFE IN MY HEART P 521, $2.25
"Style brilliant . . . and suspenseful." —*San Francisco Chronicle*

THE PRIVATE WOUND P 531, $2.25
"[Blake's] best novel in a dozen years . . . . An intensely penetrating study of sexual passion. . . . A powerful story of murder and its aftermath."
—Anthony Boucher, *New York Times*

A QUESTION OF PROOF P 494, $1.95
"The characters in this story are unusually well drawn, and the suspense is well sustained." —*New York Times*

THE SAD VARIETY P 495, $2.25
"It is a stunner. I read it instead of eating, instead of sleeping."
—Dorothy Salisbury Davis

THERE'S TROUBLE BREWING P 569, $3.37
"Nigel Strangeways is a puzzling mixture of simplicity and penetration, but all the more real for that."
—*The Times* (London) *Literary Supplement*

THOU SHELL OF DEATH P 428, $1.95
"It has all the virtues of culture, intelligence and sensibility that the most exacting connoisseur could ask of detective fiction."
—*The Times* (London) *Literary Supplement*

THE WIDOW'S CRUISE P 399, $2.25
"A stirring suspense. . . . The thrilling tale leaves nothing to be desired."
—*Springfield Republican*

Oliver Bleeck

THE BRASS GO-BETWEEN P 645, $2.84
"Fiction with a flair, well above the norm for thrillers."
—*Associated Press*

THE PROCANE CHRONICLE P 647, $2.84
"Without peer in American suspense." —*Los Angeles Times*

PROTOCOL FOR A KIDNAPPING P 646, $2.84
"The zigzags of plot are electric; the characters sharp; but it is the wit and irony and touches of plain fun which make the whole a standout."
—*Los Angeles Times*

John & Emery Bonett

A BANNER FOR PEGASUS   P 554, $2.40
"A gem! Beautifully plotted and set. . . . Not only is the murder adroit
and deserved, and the detection competent, but the love story is charm-
ing."   —Jacques Barzun and Wendell Hertig Taylor

DEAD LION   P 563, $2.40
"A clever plot, authentic background and interesting characters highly
recommended this one."   —*New Republic*

THE SOUND OF MURDER   P 642, $2.84
The suspects are many, the clues few, but the gentle Inspector ferrets out
the truth and pursues the case to its bitter and shocking end.

Christianna Brand

GREEN FOR DANGER   P 551, $2.50
"You have to reach for the greatest of Great Names (Christie, Carr,
Queen . . .) to find Brand's rivals in the devious subtleties of the trade."
                                                   —Anthony Boucher

TOUR DE FORCE   P 572, $2.40
"Complete with traps for the over-ingenious, a double-reverse surprise
ending and a key clue planted so fairly and obviously that you completely
overlook it. If that's your idea of perfect entertainment, then seize at once
upon *Tour de Force.*"   —Anthony Boucher, *New York Times*

James Byrom

OR BE HE DEAD   P 585, $2.84
"A very original tale . . . Well written and steadily entertaining."
 —Jacques Barzun and Wendell Hertig Taylor, *A Catalogue of Crime*

Henry Calvin

IT'S DIFFERENT ABROAD   P 640, $2.84
"What is remarkable and delightful, Mr. Calvin imparts a flavor of satire
to what he renovates and compels us to take straight."
                                                   —Jacques Barzun

Marjorie Carleton

VANISHED   P 559, $2.40
"Exceptional . . . a minor triumph."
 —Jacques Barzun and Wendell Hertig Taylor, *A Catalogue of Crime*

George Harmon Coxe

MURDER WITH PICTURES P 527, $2.25
"[Coxe] has hit the bull's-eye with his first shot."

—*New York Times*

Edmund Crispin

BURIED FOR PLEASURE P 506, $2.50
"Absolute and unalloyed delight."

—Anthony Boucher, *New York Times*

Lionel Davidson

THE MENORAH MEN P 592, $2.84
"Of his fellow thriller writers, only John Le Carré shows the same instinct for the viscera."

—*Chicago Tribune*

NIGHT OF WENCESLAS P 595, $2.84
"A most ingenious thriller, so enriched with style, wit, and a sense of serious comedy that it all but transcends its kind."

—*The New Yorker*

THE ROSE OF TIBET P 593, $2.84
"I hadn't realized how much I missed the genuine Adventure story . . . until I read *The Rose of Tibet*."

—Graham Greene

D. M. Devine

MY BROTHER'S KILLER P 558, $2.40
"A most enjoyable crime story which I enjoyed reading down to the last moment."

—Agatha Christie

Kenneth Fearing

THE BIG CLOCK P 500, $1.95
"It will be some time before chill-hungry clients meet again so rare a compound of irony, satire, and icy-fingered narrative. *The Big Clock* is . . . a psychothriller you won't put down." —*Weekly Book Review*

Andrew Garve

THE ASHES OF LODA P 430, $1.50
"Garve . . . embellishes a fine fast adventure story with a more credible picture of the U.S.S.R. than is offered in most thrillers."

—*New York Times Book Review*

THE CUCKOO LINE AFFAIR P 451, $1.95
". . . an agreeable and ingenious piece of work." —*The New Yorker*

A HERO FOR LEANDA
P 429, $1.50

"One can trust Mr. Garve to put a fresh twist to any situation, and the ending is really a lovely surprise." —*Manchester Guardian*

MURDER THROUGH THE LOOKING GLASS
P 449, $1.95

". . . refreshingly out-of-the-way and enjoyable . . . highly recommended to all comers." —*Saturday Review*

NO TEARS FOR HILDA
P 441, $1.95

"It starts fine and finishes finer. I got behind on breathing watching Max get not only his man but his woman, too." —*Rex Stout*

THE RIDDLE OF SAMSON
P 450, $1.95

"The story is an excellent one, the people are quite likable, and the writing is superior." —*Springfield Republican*

Michael Gilbert

BLOOD AND JUDGMENT
P 446, $1.95

"Gilbert readers need scarcely be told that the characters all come alive at first sight, and that his surpassing talent for narration enhances any plot. . . . Don't miss." —*San Francisco Chronicle*

THE BODY OF A GIRL
P 459, $1.95

"Does what a good mystery should do: open up into all kinds of ramifications, with untold menace behind the action. At the end, there is a bang-up climax, and it is a pleasure to see how skilfully Gilbert wraps everything up." —*New York Times Book Review*

FEAR TO TREAD
P 458, $1.95

"Merits serious consideration as a work of art." —*New York Times*

Joe Gores

HAMMETT
P 631, $2.84

"Joe Gores at his very best. Terse, powerful writing—with the master, Dashiell Hammett, as the protagonist in a novel I think he would have been proud to call his own." —*Robert Ludlum*

C. W. Grafton

BEYOND A REASONABLE DOUBT
P 519, $1.95

"A very ingenious tale of murder . . . a brilliant and gripping narrative." —*Jacques Barzun and Wendell Hertig Taylor*

C. W. Grafton (cont'd)

THE RAT BEGAN TO GNAW THE ROPE P 639, $2.84
"Fast, humorous story with flashes of brilliance."

—*The New Yorker*

Edward Grierson

THE SECOND MAN P 528, $2.25
"One of the best trial-testimony books to have come along in quite a while." —*The New Yorker*

Bruce Hamilton

TOO MUCH OF WATER P 635, $2.84
"A superb sea mystery. . . . The prose is excellent."
—Jacques Barzun and Wendell Hertig Taylor, *A Catalogue of Crime*

Cyril Hare

DEATH IS NO SPORTSMAN P 555, $2.40
"You will be thrilled because it succeeds in placing an ingenious story in a new and refreshing setting. . . . The identity of the murderer is really a surprise." —*Daily Mirror*

DEATH WALKS THE WOODS P 556, $2.40
"Here is a fine formal detective story, with a technically brilliant solution demanding the attention of all connoisseurs of construction."
—Anthony Boucher, *New York Times Book Review*

AN ENGLISH MURDER P 455, $2.50
"By a long shot, the best crime story I have read for a long time. Everything is traditional, but originality does not suffer. The setting is perfect. Full marks to Mr. Hare." —*Irish Press*

SUICIDE EXCEPTED P 636, $2.84
"Adroit in its manipulation . . . and distinguished by a plot-twister which I'll wager Christie wishes she'd thought of." —*New York Times*

TENANT FOR DEATH P 570, $2.84
"The way in which an air of probability is combined both with clear, terse narrative and with a good deal of subtle suburban atmosphere, proves the extreme skill of the writer." —*The Spectator*

TRAGEDY AT LAW P 522, $2.25
"An extremely urbane and well-written detective story."

—*New York Times*

Cyril Hare (cont'd)

UNTIMELY DEATH   P 514, $2.25

"The English detective story at its quiet best, meticulously underplayed, rich in perceivings of the droll human animal and ready at the last with a neat surprise which has been there all the while had we but wits to see it."   *—New York Herald Tribune Book Review*

THE WIND BLOWS DEATH   P 589, $2.84

"A plot compounded of musical knowledge, a Dickens allusion, and a subtle point in law is related with delightfully unobtrusive wit, warmth, and style."   *—New York Times*

WITH A BARE BODKIN   P 523, $2.25

"One of the best detective stories published for a long time."
     —The Spectator

Robert Harling

THE ENORMOUS SHADOW   P 545, $2.50

"In some ways the best spy story of the modern period. . . . The writing is terse and vivid . . . the ending full of action . . . altogether first-rate."
—Jacques Barzun and Wendell Hertig Taylor, *A Catalogue of Crime*

Matthew Head

THE CABINDA AFFAIR   P 541, $2.25

"An absorbing whodunit and a distinguished novel of atmosphere."
     —Anthony Boucher, *New York Times*

THE CONGO VENUS   P 597, $2.84

"Terrific. The dialogue is just plain wonderful."   *—Boston Globe*

MURDER AT THE FLEA CLUB   P 542, $2.50

"The true delight is in Head's style, its limpid ease combined with humor and an awesome precision of phrase."   *—San Francisco Chronicle*

M. V. Heberden

ENGAGED TO MURDER   P 533, $2.25

"Smooth plotting."   *—New York Times*

James Hilton

WAS IT MURDER?   P 501, $1.95

"The story is well planned and well written."   *—New York Times*

S. B. Hough

DEAR DAUGHTER DEAD P 661, $2.84

"A highly intelligent and sophisticated story of police detection . . . not to be missed on any account." —Francis Iles, *The Guardian*

SWEET SISTER SEDUCED P 662, $2.84

In the course of a nightlong conversation between the Inspector and the suspect, the complex emotions of a very strange marriage are revealed.

P. M. Hubbard

HIGH TIDE P 571, $2.40

"A smooth elaboration of mounting horror and danger."

—*Library Journal*

Elspeth Huxley

THE AFRICAN POISON MURDERS P 540, $2.25

"Obscure venom, manical mutilations, deadly bush fire, thrilling climax compose major opus.... Top-flight."

—*Saturday Review of Literature*

MURDER ON SAFARI P 587, $2.84

"Right now we'd call Mrs. Huxley a dangerous rival to Agatha Christie." —*Books*

Francis Iles

BEFORE THE FACT P 517, $2.50

"Not many 'serious' novelists have produced character studies to compare with Iles's internally terrifying portrait of the murderer in *Before the Fact,* his masterpiece and a work truly deserving the appellation of unique and beyond price." —Howard Haycraft

MALICE AFORETHOUGHT P 532, $1.95

"It is a long time since I have read anything so good as *Malice Aforethought,* with its cynical humour, acute criminology, plausible detail and rapid movement. It makes you hug yourself with pleasure."

—H. C. Harwood, *Saturday Review*

Michael Innes

APPLEBY ON ARARAT P 648, $2.84

"Superbly plotted and humorously written." —*The New Yorker*

APPLEBY'S END P 649, $2.84

"Most amusing." —*Boston Globe*

THE CASE OF THE JOURNEYING BOY   P 632, $3.12

"I could see no faults in it. There is no one to compare with him."

—*Illustrated London News*

DEATH ON A QUIET DAY   P 677, $2.84

"Delightfully witty."   —*Chicago Sunday Tribune*

DEATH BY WATER   P 574, $2.40

"The amount of ironic social criticism and deft characterization of scenes and people would serve another author for six books."

—Jacques Barzun and Wendell Hertig Taylor

HARE SITTING UP   P 590, $2.84

"There is hardly anyone (in mysteries or mainstream) more exquisitely literate, allusive and Jamesian—and hardly anyone with a firmer sense of melodramatic plot or a more vigorous gift of storytelling."

—Anthony Boucher, *New York Times*

THE LONG FAREWELL   P 575, $2.40

"A model of the deft, classic detective story, told in the most wittily diverting prose."   —*New York Times*

THE MAN FROM THE SEA   P 591, $2.84

"The pace is brisk, the adventures exciting and excitingly told, and above all he keeps to the very end the interesting ambiguity of the man from the sea."   —*New Statesman*

ONE MAN SHOW   P 672, $2.84

"Exciting, amusingly written . . . very good enjoyment it is."

—*The Spectator*

THE SECRET VANGUARD   P 584, $2.84

"Innes . . . has mastered the art of swift, exciting and well-organized narrative."   —*New York Times*

THE WEIGHT OF THE EVIDENCE   P 633, $2.84

"First-class puzzle, deftly solved. University background interesting and amusing."   —*Saturday Review of Literature*

Mary Kelly

THE SPOILT KILL   P 565, $2.40

"Mary Kelly is a new Dorothy Sayers. . . . [An] exciting new novel."

—*Evening News*

Lange Lewis

THE BIRTHDAY MURDER P 518, $1.95
"Almost perfect in its playlike purity and delightful prose."
—Jacques Barzun and Wendell Hertig Taylor

Allan MacKinnon

HOUSE OF DARKNESS P 582, $2.84
"His best . . . a perfect compendium."
—Jacques Barzun and Wendell Hertig Taylor, *A Catalogue of Crime*

Frank Parrish

FIRE IN THE BARLEY P 651, $2.84
"A remarkable and brilliant first novel. . . . entrancing."
—*The Spectator*

SNARE IN THE DARK P 650, $2.84
The wily English poacher Dan Mallett is framed for murder and has to confront unknown enemies to clear himself.

STING OF THE HONEYBEE P 652, $2.84
"Terrorism and murder visit a sleepy English village in this witty, offbeat thriller."
—*Chicago Sun-Times*

Austin Ripley

MINUTE MYSTERIES P 387, $2.50
More than one hundred of the world's shortest detective stories. Only one possible solution to each case!

Thomas Sterling

THE EVIL OF THE DAY P 529, $2.50
"Prose as witty and subtle as it is sharp and clear. . .characters unconventionally conceived and richly bodied forth . . . . In short, a novel to be treasured."
—Anthony Boucher, *New York Times*

Julian Symons

THE BELTING INHERITANCE P 468, $1.95
"A superb whodunit in the best tradition of the detective story."
—August Derleth, *Madison Capital Times*

BOGUE'S FORTUNE P 481, $1.95
"There's a touch of the old sardonic humour, and more than a touch of style."
—*The Spectator*

Julian Symons (cont'd)

THE COLOR OF MURDER P 461, $1.95

"A singularly unostentatious and memorably brilliant detective story."
—*New York Herald Tribune Book Review*

Dorothy Stockbridge Tillet
(John Stephen Strange)

THE MAN WHO KILLED FORTESCUE P 536, $2.25

"Better than average." —*Saturday Review of Literature*

Simon Troy

THE ROAD TO RHUINE P 583, $2.84

"Unusual and agreeably told." —*San Francisco Chronicle*

SWIFT TO ITS CLOSE P 546, $2.40

"A nicely literate British mystery . . . the atmosphere and the plot are
exceptionally well wrought, the dialogue excellent." —*Best Sellers*

Henry Wade

THE DUKE OF YORK'S STEPS P 588, $2.84

"A classic of the golden age."
—Jacques Barzun and Wendell Hertig Taylor, *A Catalogue of Crime*

A DYING FALL P 543, $2.50

"One of those expert British suspense jobs . . . it crackles with undercur-
rents of blackmail, violent passion and murder. Topnotch in its class."
—*Time*

THE HANGING CAPTAIN P 548, $2.50

"This is a detective story for connoisseurs, for those who value clear
thinking and good writing above mere ingenuity and easy thrills."
—*The Times* (London) *Literary Supplement*

Hillary Waugh

LAST SEEN WEARING . . . P 552, $2.40

"A brilliant tour de force." —Julian Symons

THE MISSING MAN P 553, $2.40

"The quiet detailed police work of Chief Fred C. Fellows, Stockford,
Conn., is at its best in *The Missing Man* . . . one of the Chief's toughest
cases and one of the best handled."

—Anthony Boucher, *New York Times Book Review*

Henry Kitchell Webster

WHO IS THE NEXT?   P 539, $2.25

"A double murder, private-plane piloting, a neat impersonation, and a delicate courtship are adroitly combined by a writer who knows how to use the language." —Jacques Barzun and Wendell Hertig Taylor

John Welcome

GO FOR BROKE   P 663, $2.84

A rich financier chases Richard Graham half 'round Europe in a desperate attempt to prevent the truth getting out.

RUN FOR COVER   P 664, $2.84

"I can think of few writers in the international intrigue game with such a gift for fast and vivid storytelling."

—*New York Times Book Review*

STOP AT NOTHING   P 665, $2.84

"Mr. Welcome is lively, vivid and highly readable."

—*New York Times Book Review*

Anna Mary Wells

MURDERER'S CHOICE   P 534, $2.50

"Good writing, ample action, and excellent character work."

—*Saturday Review of Literature*

A TALENT FOR MURDER   P 535, $2.25

"The discovery of the villain is a decided shock."   —*Books*

Charles Williams

DEAD CALM   P 655, $2.84

"A brilliant tour de force of inventive plotting, fine manipulation of a small cast and breathtaking sequences of spectacular navigation."

—*New York Times Book Review*

THE SAILCLOTH SHROUD   P 654, $2.84

"A fine novel of excitement, spirited, fresh and satisfying."

—*New York Times*

THE WRONG VENUS   P 656, $2.84

Swindler Lawrence Colby and the lovely Martine create a story of romance, larceny, and very blunt homicide.

Edward Young

THE FIFTH PASSENGER

P 544, $2.25

"Clever and adroit . . . excellent thriller. . . ." 　—*Library Journal*

If you enjoyed this book you'll want to know about
THE PERENNIAL LIBRARY MYSTERY SERIES
Buy them at your local bookstore or use this coupon for ordering:

Qty	P number	Price

	postage and handling charge	$1.00
_____ book(s) @ $0.25		
	TOTAL	

Prices contained in this coupon are Harper & Row invoice prices only. They are subject to change without notice, and in no way reflect the prices at which these books may be sold by other suppliers.

HARPER & ROW, Mail Order Dept. #PMS, 10 East 53rd St., New York, N.Y. 10022.

Please send me the books I have checked above. I am enclosing $_____ which includes a postage and handling charge of $1.00 for the first book and 25¢ for each additional book. Send check or money order. No cash or C.O.D.s please

Name_____

Address_____

City_____ State_____ Zip_____

Please allow 4 weeks for delivery. USA only. This offer expires 8/31/86. Please add applicable sales tax.